CLOSED
RANGE

CLOSED RANGE

BLISS LOMAX

M. EVANS

Lanham • Boulder • New York • Toronto • Plymouth, UK

Published by M. Evans
An imprint of Rowman & Littlefield
4501 Forbes Boulevard, Suite 200, Lanham, Maryland 20706
www.rowman.com

10 Thornbury Road, Plymouth PL6 7PP, United Kingdom

Distributed by National Book Network

British Library Cataloguing in Publication Information Available

Library of Congress Cataloging-in-Publication Data

Library of Congress Control Number: 2014942916
ISBN: 978-1-59077-426-7 (pbk. : alk. paper)
ISBN: 978-1-59077-427-4 (electronic)

∞™ The paper used in this publication meets the minimum requirements of
American National Standard for Information Sciences—Permanence of
Paper for Printed Library Materials, ANSI/NISO Z39.48-1992.

Printed in the United States of America

CONTENTS

CONTENTS

CLOSED RANGE

CHAPTER ONE

ON THE BOZEMAN TRAIL

WYOMING was yet the wild and perilous home of the roving Sioux, Cheyenne and Arapahoe when the Osage orange-wood wheels of thousands of "Murphy" wagons first rutted the lonely prairie road to Montana that Jess Catlin and his bawling Pitchfork trail-herd followed south this hot, dry, blinding afternoon in August.

Wave after undulating wave, the upland plains stretched away, shimmering in the heat blast and carpeted with short, curly buffalo grass in cured tufts.

The trail itself was hockdeep in feathery alkali dust which rose in glinting, golden clouds under the hoofs of the plodding steers, powdering their hides and stinging the eyes and parching the nostrils and throats of both man and beast.

The outfit was a small one of five riders, four of whom were Catlins. The fifth, Smoke Chaloner, hazed the *caballado* along behind the herd.

Bawling their thirst and torment, the Pitchfork steers were docile from weariness, stretching out for more than half-a-mile and tramping steadily with a dull rumble of hoofs. Sweat creased their dust-caked hides with dark rivulets. Their rolling, worried eyes were piteous. Riding the right flank, from time to time,

Jess Catlin swung in his saddle, a hand on the piebald's rump, judging the condition of his stock. It was plain that a halt must be made soon if he wanted to leave more than a few stringy pounds of beef on any of them.

The eldest of the family at thirty-seven, and its head, Jess had the prominent jaw and keen, disconcerting gaze of the Catlins. A six-footer, he possessed the strong frame and easy seat of a born horseman. Since early childhood his days had been spent in following the hardy long-horns, but he had not left behind him the quiet reserve of his native Kentucky, nor the fierce independence of that heritage. There was an air of brusque competence about him that bespoke a just severity in all his acts.

"Must be gittin' nigh to Fetterman," he muttered, noting the sparse clumps of sagebrush which that morning had been non-existent along the slopes.

Oblivious of discomfort, Jess stared about in search of distant cottonwoods in the folds of the land that indicated lurking water, or studied the available forage. There was nothing in his mind save the care and safety of the herd.

Across the tossing sea of horns, his brother Billy slouched in the saddle with deceptive indolence. Billy was five years younger than Jess, slighter and not so tall, but with a body of whale-bone toughness. Though no fool, he liked show and wore a checked shirt and two bone-handled forty-fives in open-end, cutaway holsters.

His dusty Stetson was tilted forward now, his kerchief over his perspiring face. His blue eyes held an indomitable good-nature as he squinted at the sun, dim and red through the blanketing fog of dust. He longed for a smoke, but knew its uselessness—the bitterness of tobacco in such a smudge. He sighed, wiping his brow with upraised arm as he glanced back.

"Hey-up, there! Git along—you blasted long-horn snails!" The cry came from far down the winding, black-and-brindled herd.

At the rear, in the hottest, dirtiest position, Glen Catlin, the youngest of the brothers, prodded the laggards and calves with intent absorption in his task. His clothes were heavy with dust, and his every movement set free a thickening cloud of it. His lashes and brows and hair were powdered white, his lips caked and burning. His bronc was in a fractious lather. Holding it in with iron grip, he waved his coiled rope and raised his voice in constant shrill adjuration.

Half-a-mile behind the *caballado,* out of the rolling alkali dust, followed the camp wagon—a veritable travelling ranch house, tall and cumbrous, with its little windows, the paint chipping from its weathered sides. The Catlins were free-rangers, as their father, "Old Blue Grass," had been before them.

Red, the Shoshone youth, hunched on the swaying seat behind the mules with the lines slack in his grasp, and appeared asleep. But he was not asleep. Under the bronze, impassive features and slitted black eyes lurked an inscrutable awareness. His gaze did not remove from the low, clotted cloud that crawled ahead.

A mile away and in front of that cloud, riding point in the clean sparkling air, Rhoda Catlin sat on her *palomino* with the unconscious grace of youth. She rode astride, erect and free, without irk in the flannel shirt and blue overalls she wore; her small hands gloved, her feet soft-booted and trim.

It was not solely for freedom from grime that Rhoda had been placed at the head of the Pitchfork herd. She was as good a puncher as her brothers, her experience curtailed only by the span of her score of years. Taking her place with the rest, in a world which knew no room for frills and ribbons, she had ridden on round-up since earliest pig-tail days, and carried a coiled rope as proudly and wielded it as effectively as any.

If she had lost anything of femininity thereby, it was not discernible. In her the dominant characteristics of the Catlins were softened without weakness. Her brown wavy hair framed a face of full curves in which self-possession reposed. Perspiration delicately beaded her smooth tan brow. Her hazel eyes were calm as she scanned the prairie with comprehensive sweep.

She was not unaware of the solitude and the great peace in which the bawling of steers, their muffled thunder, and the cries of her brother Glen echoed and were lost. Once, at the panicky snort of the *palomino*, she shot the head off a buzzing rattlesnake without aversion. She saw with pleasure the scampering prairie

dogs and the pale antelope, moving ahead; and even
the solitary coyote that watched from a knoll this
creeping invasion of his silence.

Twenty years had passed since the first ox-team
lumbered over the Bozeman Trail. The pride of Sitting Bull and Red Cloud, Crazy Horse and the rest
of that fierce company had at length been humbled.
On this broad, mountain-tapestried range, the last
stand of the northern buffalo herds had been made
and lost. Wyoming had been spanned by the Union
Pacific railroad more than a dozen years before.

Still the country remained raw, wild, new. The
towns of the Territory could be counted on the fingers
of one hand. Not all the military posts of the Mountain
District had been abandoned, nor even most of them.

Time had been, for a few brief years, when all men
were honest and hard-working; most of them known
to one another, and ever ready with helping hand.
That had been a brawny, lonesome, and withal, benefi-
cent life. Except for the inevitable enmities, to say
'cowman' was to say 'brother.' Range was free and
cattle cheap. It had been during that time that "Old
Blue Grass" Catlin had passed away, full of years and
of confidence in the heritage he handed on to his children.

But those days were gone. A new yeast was working
far in the south. Every season cattle were pouring

into the Territory over the trails from Texas; and not only cattle but, to the west and south, the swarming herds of sheepmen. And with the tide came restless scores of cowboys and herders, stage-robbers and home-seekers, gamblers and rustlers and cattle agents, following the blue-clad cavalry but, in the main, ahead of law and order.

Wyoming had become another country overnight— a land in which men were a law unto themselves.

Although the older stockmen still clung together they were being divided by new loyalties, under the pressure of altering circumstances. Eastern and foreign capital was erecting vast baronetcies in the midst of freehold. Small nesters, disdaining the old order of the free range, squatted and built up their herds by stealth.

The gradual, turbulent settlement of the range had begun. Fierce wars arose, flickered, and died down. Men fought for the choicer ranch sites, and sometimes died. Rustlers preyed on the unwary. Near the railroad towns and stage stations to the south, guards were imperative. No man was accounted a friend until he had declared himself. Skulkers were shot at, and the red-handed hung, if they could be caught. It was a stern policy, but necessary.

Although little sign of the lamentable condition was visible this afternoon on the Bozeman Trail, Jess Catlin was aware of it. Rhoda too, was thinking of it gravely as she gazed at a small, elongated blot far ahead, silhouetted against the brassy sky.

The distance was too great for identification, but she judged it to be a band of horsemen, advancing along the sinuous trail. She glanced back distractedly, and was startled by the near approach of Jess. He was peering intently forward.

In another moment the mysterious blot dropped down a gentle slope and was lost to view.

"Wha'd yuh make of it?" Jess queried gruffly. "Punchers?"

"I couldn't be sure, Jess. It looked like horses, and yet——" Her voice was low, rich, modulated.

He appeared undecided, staring back over the plodding herd. "If they're cowmen, you drop back an' leave me point," he told her finally. "An' if anythin' starts, go after Red, pronto. You hear?"

She assented, meeting his strict scrutiny untroubledly.

"I was agoin' to swing off for Poison Spider Creek," Jess went on uneasily, "but I won't have it look as though we was runnin'. We'll jest wait till we get past this——" He broke off, gazing ahead again. "Mebbe it's a bunch of Shoshones goin' to Washakie," he added without conviction.

For long minutes they rode knee to knee in silence. Then over a nearer swell rose the figures of two horsemen in a similar position. Billy Catlin saw them also. He started to work forward along the Pitchfork herd. Jess waved him back impatiently.

Behind the approaching riders appeared horses, not bunched, but in a double line; and behind them, another brace of mounted men. Dust obscured the twinkling legs, boiling low and soon left behind in the rapid advance. Jess Catlin grunted, his interest lapsing as he identified the cavalry uniforms of the guards.

"Bunch of sojers takin' a cavvieyard up to Fort Mc-Kinney," he commented shortly.

Rhoda, however, continued to gaze with attention. Her eyes were admiring as the cavalrymen drew near at a road gait and she noted the free, wild spirit of the horses. There must have been fifty of them in the bunch. They were haltered at intervals to a long rope suspended between the harnessed teams in front and rear.

She spared a glance at the soldiers as they swung out to pass around the Pitchfork herd. They sat erect and alert in the military saddles. One of them lifted a greeting hand to Jess, and flashed a smile at Rhoda which she returned. Then her gaze went back to the horses, rushing past. A few were spooky, but nearly all were superb animals, with pricked ears and high heads. Their hoofs rolled, kicking up the powdery alkali. In a moment they were gone, and the prairie ahead was empty, silent, slumbering under the declining afternoon sun.

Jess Catlin had, in the meantime, made up his mind

to some purpose. He waved Billy forward with an imperative gesture.

"We'll swing west an' hit Lost Cabin Creek," he said, when the latter came alongside. "Ought to find some good range in there. We c'n let 'em graze for a week or two, an' sound out the country below. No use over-reachin' ourselves. But it should rain in a few days, an' we'll be all right." His hard eye scanned the cloudless, metallic sky as he ended. It would have been impossible to tell by what sign he judged.

Working in unison, the three expertly swung the head of the herd out upon the open plains. The steers swerved reluctantly, the rangy brutes in the lead tossing their horns and making repeated breaks for freedom. The riders turned them back, enforcing an inexorable patience, their ponies glistening and winded. At length the herd straightened out in the new direction.

Here the dust was less dense, though it still rose in a curling, feathered wave twenty feet high. The Catlins sighed their relief. Even Smoke Chaloner's eye lighted up as he turned the broncs.

The orange sun was lowering toward the faint blue demarcation of the Big Horns when the cattle finally smelt water and began to press forward at a loggy trot, bellowing their relief and desire. Beyond a gentle rise the ground fell away in a long gradient to the creek. The Pitchfork steers spread out and lumbered toward the stream in an accelerating billow.

As he helped Billy and Glen haze the last of the herd

forward Jess Catlin noted with satisfaction that here the buffalo and grama grass were fairly luxuriant. He rode out on the crest of the grassy swell and drew up; and only then the genial light in his eyes faded, his lips sternly compressed.

"Whut in tarnation hell's this, now?" he burst out wrathfully.

Spread along both sides of Lost Cabin Creek, their curious heads raised, were better than a hundred strange steers toward which the Pitchfork cows were hurtling with unabated enthusiasm and amongst which they must inevitably mix, to the confusion of both herds.

CHAPTER TWO

AUGUST RAIN

"THEY'RE J B steers, with a dewlap earmark!" called Glen Catlin, riding slowly toward Jess.

"J B *and* Pitchfork steers, now!" sang out Billy disgustedly, drawing rein and peering keenly at his older brother. "D'you recognize the brand, Jess?"

Pulled up at one side, Rhoda gazed at her brothers anxiously. Smoke Chaloner was hazing the horses to water farther up the creek and surveying the intermingled herds with impassive sobriety.

"Can't say I do," Jess responded laconically. "Some small outfit likely. Whoever 'tis 'll be down at Lost Cabin."

Billy started away immediately, spurring his jaded pony into a bound. "That's soon looked into! We'll get 'em on the run before they come up here an' jump us!" His usually cheerful face was sharp and grim.

"Come back hyar!" Jess commanded severely. "You ain't goin' nowhar with a chip on yore shoulder!"

Billy jerked the rein intolerantly. "What're we goin' to do—cut our stuff out an' breeze 'em along, like lost dogs?" he snapped.

"No! We'll go down an' see this party. But you won't be in the lead, an' you c'n jest fergit about it!" Jess turned to Rhoda. "You an' Smoke keep an' eye peeled, Rho. An' throw together a bait soon's Red gits here. We'll be back fer it . . . C'mon, Glen."

Together the men rode down the grassy bank.

"Hell of a note!" Billy complained indignantly. "Range is gittin' all cluttered up with folks insistin' on this, an' grabbin' that! 'Nother two years an' there won't be no free water you c'n git to! An' I bet this bird'll go to *claim* the creek on you . . . What'll we do if he's on the peck about it?"

"Then you c'n tie into him!" Jess retorted tersely.

In ten minutes they came within sight of the tumble-down sod shanty known as Lost Cabin. For years it had stood on the stream bank, tenanted infrequently by passing cowboys. This evening smoke drifted thinly from the pierced roof, and behind the cabin stood a wagon and a pony with hanging head.

The sound of lashing spray as the Catlins forded the creek brought a man to the door. He stepped out, a long-barreled rifle in his grasp. They saw that he was past the fifty mark, tall and bearded, his gaze sharp and his manner shrewd and ready.

"Howdy, strangers," he nodded as they rode up. He did not invite them to dismount, scrutinizing them carefully, one by one.

"Livin' hyar?" Jess inquired gruffly.

"Yeh." The beard barely moved, below the bright gaze. "Runnin' a few cows up the creek. Name's Brush."

"Joe!" a feminine but ungentle voice reprimanded

from within. "Don't you go tellin' all you know!" Apprehension twanged in the words.

Brush made no rejoinder; his regard did not waver.

Jess Catlin nodded. "We're Catlins," he returned evenly. *"We're* runnin' cows up the creek. Free-rangin' . . . Pitchfork outfit." It was at once announcement and challenge.

"I've heard o' you," Brush admitted, relaxing slightly. He started to lean the rifle against the shanty, then thought better of it. "I got no objections," he went on, "long as you don't oust my stock."

Still Jess remained undecided, his face cold and strict.

"Squattin' hyar, eh?" he persisted curtly.

"Yes!" There was no uncertainty in that explosive answer. Brush's face began to cloud. "Why not? Catlin, thar's big outfits south of hyar, takin' up fifteen-twenty squar miles o' range at a clip! I tell you it's gittin' so a man's got to grab or come out on the small end! . . . If I war you-all——"

Billy flared impatiently: "If you was us, Brush, you'd stuck to yore buffalo gun, an' not got married!"

A venomous snort sounded from within the sod shanty.

"Billy!" Glen exclaimed sharply. Jess silenced them both with a gesture.

"Whut big outfits you referrin' to?" he went on soberly to Brush.

"Why, the Tincup! Them an' the Spade brand 've hogged near everythin' from hyar to the railroad!"

The Catlins knew both spreads; the latter an English investment running into many thousand head of cattle, and rapidly expanding; the former the outfit of Colonel Purdy, many of whose cowboys they knew well. They listened noncommittally while Brush continued in a vindictive tone:

"The Spade layout's brought some cocky young cub over hyar from the old country this season, an' he's jest plumb full o' bright notions . . . Silver-mounted spurs an' postage-stamp saddles! Blooded prize stock-breeders, an' eastern hay!" He shot a jet of tobacco-juice into the dust, and the black beard jutted contemptuously.

"Has he been tellin' you whut to do?" Jess demanded.

"He's be'n tellin' me whut not to do!" Brush growled angrily. He cursed the overseas interloper with heat.

Jess withdrew from the subject disinterestedly, his gaze nervous. "Wal, we'll mog back to our wagon," he decided. "I guess you an' me'll pinch along somehow. Our cows're pretty well mixed right now, but we'll cut out yore stuff before we drift south . . . An' Brush, when you shoot a head fer beef, you hunt yore own brand!" He glanced sharply.

"Shore!" the buffalo-hunter agreed readily; then he paused to stare, caught by the suspicion that Catlin was implying more than he need. He said nothing, watching narrowly as the brothers swung their ponies away.

Massed ruby clouds had piled up in the south and west, above which the sun hovered brilliantly red. The range was lighted up with an atmospheric effulgence in which the herd, as the Catlins neared, grazed stolidly, touched with glowing tints. Prairie chickens cackled sleepily.

Red had come up with the camp wagon—"Catlin's dog-house," it was called by dozens of isolated range men who recognized it from afar—and Rhoda had the evening meal prepared.

The girl watched her brothers free their mounts and tramp in on tottering high heels, to squat near the fire, plates on their laps and steaming cups beside them on the ground. Only after hunger had been appeased did she venture to inquire concerning their visit to Lost Cabin.

Glen told her, his eye lighting up with approval as he noted that Rhoda had rearranged her soft, flowing hair and slipped into a plain but attractive dress.

"You look nice, Rhoda," he interrupted his story to remark. It struck him as unusual that Rhoda had not succumbed, despite her rude and active life, to the dowdy, hopeless plainness of most of the women-folk of the country.

"Do you think so?" she smiled gently.

She was pleased with his good opinion. Of all her brothers, Glen was the only one with whom she enjoyed a real community of understanding. To him alone she could look for anything beyond absent-minded tolerance. They were still chatting when Jess and Billy rode up to the wagon once more, having thrown their saddles on fresh horses.

"Where're you two goin'?" Glen stood up to inquire.

"Fetterman," Jess answered, reaching down to tug his saddle-boot into an easier position. "Be back 'fore mornin'." His tone was absently evasive. But beyond the withers of his pony, Billy's eyes shone with a suspicious brightness. Glen only nodded.

"I don't know as it's necessary for 'em to go there tonight," he said slowly, a minute later, watching his brothers' diminishing figures. "Fetterman's full of hard-cases an' riffraff. It don't help to advertise yoreself to them . . . Smoke's rolled in his soogan right now, an' we'll follow him soon enough."

"They can take care of themselves," Rhoda told him untroubledly.

"They can—sober," he responded bluntly. "Jess knows when to stop. But Billy's been itchin' to howl for days!"

Taught by experience, Rhoda had no more to say. Glen helped her wash the dirty plates and pans. As dusk settled, he slapped at mosquitos and buffalo gnats as vigorously as she, but his face remained thoughtful.

Far out on the darkening range, Red, the Shoshone youth, moved in a slow curve, taking the first trick of the night guard. Heat lightning flickered along the horizon. The solitude was profound.

Retiring to her bunk in the "dog-house," Rhoda was grateful to providence for the existence of her brother Glen. Only a year older than herself, he appeared the most sensible member of the family. He would, Rhoda felt, have liked also to go to Fetterman. But he did not rush away in the first few minutes from a camp at which they were likely to stay for some time, perhaps weeks.

There was, to be sure, ample reason for any of them to seek relaxation. Behind them lay months of loneliness in the north, beyond Powder River in the shadow of the Big Horns. On that secluded range they had wintered in a dugout, caring for the Pitchfork cattle through long days of bitter temperatures in which the weakened animals died, and tempers grew short and taut.

With every howling storm the steers had drifted before the blast, roaming the inhospitable prairie like lost souls. Many a ride carried the guards miles to the south. It was a drift, however, that was to be more deliberate. Only now, under the weight of summer heat and drought, did Jess Catlin lead the slow trek, with many a halt for rest and grazing, that would find the herd fat and sleek near the shipping-point of Medicine Bow in early fall.

It was an iron programme from which men revolted periodically. Billy was liable to explode violently; Jess perhaps more cautiously, with an inward effect. Both Glen and Rhoda would go to town more for diversion than anything else.

Red, the Shoshone, appeared immune to the necessities of his white-skinned companions. And Smoke

Chaloner indulged a spree about once yearly, disappearing on some plausible pretext for a week, for two weeks, to return haggard and drawn, chastened in manner, quieter than ever, and penniless.

Thinking about these things, Rhoda dozed off into dreamless sleep. She was aroused sometime later by Glen's pounding on the thin wall of her bunk, and started up, attracted by the ghostly flutter of the dishtowel window curtains and the persistent, heavy drumming of rain on the roof. Low thunder rumbled sullenly through the pitch-black night.

"Climb out, Rho!" Glen called urgently. "Herd's pretty restless!"

"Are Jess and Billy back?" she demanded, leaning on her elbow, her faculties fully awake.

"No . . . I'm leavin' a pony out here for you. Get with it, kid!"

She heard his mount pound away, and leaped from her bunk hastily to don her riding garb and an old slouch hat.

Cool rain met her face as she stepped out. The storm was not far advanced, which accounted for her not having awakened; nor was the ground yet soggy. The wind soughed premonitorily, tugging at her hat, and shredding the songs of Glen and Chaloner wafted from the direction of the herd.

As Rhoda yanked up the latigo and swung into the saddle, protracted lightning fanged the sky. In the blackness which followed, she jumped the pony toward the creek and splashed through, trusting to

the animal's instinct for safety. The rain came down
with a steady increase in volume, pelting and heavy.

Another blaze of lightning ripped the night and
showed her the milling herd. Already half-a-mile
below the creek, it was restless and drifting. Deafening
thunder boomed as she pushed hurriedly forward to
take her part in keeping the cattle bunched and under
control.

On the other side of the herd Glen Catlin pressed
steadily against the southward drift, trying to turn
the steers. They tossed their heads and broke re-
peatedly, lunging toward freedom. Flash after flash of
vivid light revealed their hides soaked and running;
horns glistening, eyes wide and fearful.

It was a strenuous task, keeping them turned back.
Glen cut them off sharply, his coiled rope swishing.
Red was busy near by. Save for the lightning, they
strove blindly.

The lightning increased in vicious frequency; the
crashing reverberations were almost endless. Only at
intervals could the singing be heard—Rhoda's strong,
full voice rising above the pound of hoofs and click
of horns.

During one bright flash Glen caught a glimpse of
another rider. It was Joe Brush, aroused by the storm
and magnanimously—or cautiously—come to aid with
the frightened stock. His dark beard was stringy with
rain, his mustache drooping.

Glen's attention returned to the steers. "Jess'll
sweat some over this, bein' away," he thought grimly,

trying to estimate the probable duration of the storm. "For once he won't know what's goin' on!"

Already he was hot and wearied. His pony's breathing was labored. Others were in no better case. Yet perhaps nothing would have come of the night's elemental disturbance had it not been for the high electrical tensity of the air.

In a low grama-sown swale less than a quarter of a mile from the herd there appeared an eery, hovering ball of fire, luminous and brilliant. Glen's exasperated curse stuck in his throat as he saw it.

The steers spied it at the same instant. Many rose fighting on hind legs, and then dropped to plunge madly forward. Deep snorts and bawls of unqualified fear rent the night above the sullen voice of the clouds.

An irresistible wave of crazed cattle swept about the helpless punchers and thundered away into the darkness. The ironic salute of a belated bolt revealed a furious sea of bounding humps and waving horns which it was useless to attempt to stem.

CHAPTER THREE

FETTERMAN NIGHTS

FETTERMAN after sundown, wild and raucous and unregenerate, held an intoxicant quality to which few failed to respond. In its unaccustomed aura Billy Catlin's step was light and expectant. He was untouched by the slow, thoughtful caution that invested his brother's manner as they moved in pursuit of a drink with the common impulse of long thirst.

In the Orpha saloon they found both bar space and old acquaintances. Hank Chiles, a grizzled free-ranger in a tattered vest, slapped Jess heartily on the shoulder.

"Daggone it, Catlin, here we are in the middle of summer ag'in!" he exclaimed with a show of cordiality. "How'd you winter?"

Jess shook his head. "Lost half my calf-crop, Hank. Dunno how a man c'n kick though, with prices whar they are now."

Chiles dubiously agreed. "We come through better'n lots of folks. Trouble is, Catlin, the south range is over-stocked from Colorado to Texas! They make their own bad winters, grazin' the country bare like they're doin'! An' they'll be makin' 'em for us too, crowdin' in here!"

Jess considered this soberly, sipping his drink. "Wal, I guess thar's room 'nough for all," he thought.

"No!" Chiles insisted. "Catlin, that's where yo're wrong! Three-four years ago a long-horn was a sight to see. Since then there's half-a-million steers gone up th' trail to Montana!"

Jess listened with bent head, his gaze vacant, but unconvinced, as Chiles' indictment ran on.

At their side, Billy and one of Chiles' cowboys were interested in more lively topics. Billy downed three fingers at a gulp and turned to watch the varied scene going on around him. Everywhere men nodded over drinks, deep in discussion. Cowboys pranked and clowned. The card tables were well attended; many with rings of spectators.

"Man, this neck o' woods is pickin' up!" Bitter Creek confided knowingly. "There was a man shot plumb in front of the Cheyenne Club, day-so ago. Rubbed 'is spurs round on them slick rugs they got inside, an' the bouncer got peeved. An' it ain't a week since they lynched a feller jest outside Lusk," he went on. "That Texas trail is shore hummin'!"

Billy nodded complacently. "That goes fer the Bozeman road too. Folks hittin' for the gold diggin's in the Black Hills."

"Yeah. An' they wind up huntin' fer jobs on the Northern Pacific!" Bitter Creek guffawed. ". . . Wal, it don't make. You play 'round a while, an' then you cash yore chips. 'Member young Lash, in our outfit? He's gone. Catched the cholera over on the Belle Fourche, an' we planted 'im."

Billy's frown was fleeting. "That cholera's bad.

Dunno but I'd as soon ketch that as the tick fever though."

Bitter Creek grinned: "Look. When you find a tick on you, you jest light a match an' hold it 'longside the critter's tail. It'll back right out, head an' all! . . . This knockin' 'em off accidental is what hurts. The head busts off inside you, an' starts the fever."

"I don' wanto know nothin' about 'em!" Billy rejoined good-naturedly. "Let's have 'nother drink."

They turned back to the bar, glancing at Chiles and Jess, who were still involved in their talk.

"I didn't want nothin' to *do* with the Spade outfit, so I stuck close to the flat," Hank was saying gruffly; "but this blame beef-eater Mackey sends a man out there couple times to 'warn' me!"

Jess harkened closely, remembering what Joe Brush had said concerning the English syndicate. "Warn you?" he echoed puzzledly.

"Yeh! He sent me word I was to keep my herd away from the Boxelder," Hank went on angrily. "Claims his blooded Illinoy bulls'll git the Texas fever from my steers!"

"Wal, I hear the stock's fadin' away back thar from pneumonia," Jess commented dryly.

"Shore! It's jest as broad as 'tis long! But Catlin, if their game works, they'll jest plumb keep us north o' the Platte!"

"I guess they won't!" Jess hazardly grimly. "Come shippin' time, anyway!"

"But why should they any time atall?" Hank demanded heatedly. "I don't need much in the way of range; but what I want, I'll have! But you *can't* get 'long with some tarnation plush-covered knothead that don' even know the business! Why Catlin, after I cussed 'is man out, Mackey come foggin' out there to the flat an' offered me twenty dollars apiece fer every head I've got!"

Jess pierced him with a glance. "Why didn't you sell, an' hit south fer 'nother bunch? No feeder c'n make money at that price!"

"I *know* it!" Chiles' brows were corrugated. "Jess, it ain't a question of feedin'. It's one of land! I wouldn' sell my grazin' rights fer a hundred a head on all I've got! . . . Mackey made that offer to git rid o' me!"

Jess frowned his disapproval of the possibility. "Wal, I 'low you got the beef-eater wrong, Hank."

"That may be. Lord knows *I* don't want no ruckus. But it's a case of us free grass men havin' to stand together. If you run acrost any others, why, talk to 'em! It's what I'm doin'!"

"That's sense," Jess conceded weightily.

"And it don't have to be only free-rangers either," Hank pursued. "It's the big feller against the little feller; an' here's once we'll win if it takes the hoe men to help us!"

Jess shook his head disparagingly. "You c'n count me out of that. I won't help no granger ag'in a cowman!"

They argued it pro and con; Chiles with flashing eyes, Jess with habitual hard caution. Listening with bent heads, Billy and Bitter Creek nodded from time to time, meeting each other's glance.

Putting down the glass after his fifth drink, Billy would have commented had he not been interrupted by a disturbance down the bar. He paused, wavering slightly, to stare in the direction from which the commotion sounded.

A big man with flushed face, hat on the back of his head, was violently cursing another man who tried to pass it off. The big man was determined he would not pass it off.

"That's Van Wagoner," Bitter Creek volunteered. "Come up from Texas couple weeks ago. . . . Ain't he windy?"

Billy nodded judiciously. He was beginning to feel the effects of his drinking. "Windy's hell," he decided. "Don' like him a bit." He turned back to resume his interrupted discourse. His mouth was open to speak when another snarling roar from Wagoner halted him. Billy swung around wrathfully. "Hey, down there! Bottle it, blast you!" he bawled.

Jess jerked him an admonishing look, but Van Wagoner paid no attention at all. He was looking for trouble. Billy stared his brother down and returned to a contemptuous examination of the bad man.

"He's hard, eh? Texan, eh?" he demanded of Bitter Creek, swaying slightly.

"He's them things orright," the latter agreed dryly.

Billy looked at him with flinty eyes as he made his.

decision. "Wal, I'll soften 'em up, an' make him from Wyomin'!" His face was ugly.

"You'll stay whar you are!" Jess thrust in dominantly, grasping his arm.

Billy threw him off. He almost lost his balance. Catching himself, he started down the bar, only to trip over the feet of a puncher and crash to the floor. He was up instantly, his features contorted with rage.

"What the hell d'you mean, trippin' me?" he blazed. "Who're you, anyhow?"

"Aw, go on an' tend to yore knittin', you damn drunk!" the puncher retorted scathingly.

"It's Gene Rule!" Bitter Creek vociferated. "He's a Spade man—likely been listenin' all along!" He flashed a warning look at Chiles and Jess Catlin.

Hank wheeled to glare at Rule. The cowboy had eyes only for Billy, who faced him threateningly, ready for the first hostile move. At this moment another puncher brushed forward to stand beside Rule, his features harsh and frowning. Two guns swung at his hips.

"Denny Jackson!" Bitter Creek ejaculated excitedly. "By God, the Spade outfit's gangin' up on us!"

Half the men in the saloon turned to gaze. Those nearest began to edge away.

Jess Catlin took command of the situation with no uncertain grasp. "Lay off!" he droned, thrushing Bitter Creek back. "We won't have no battle if I know it! Jackson—if that's yore name—that goes for you too!" His hand lay warningly on Hank Chiles' arm. "Billy!" he snapped.

"Go to hell!" that individual advised vindictively, without turning his gaze. "This here galoot wants a battle, an' he's goin' to git it!"

All his befogged indolence had dropped from him. Scarcely had he ceased speaking when his hard fist lashed out. It met Rule's jaw with sodden impact. The puncher's head snapped back and he howled unintelligibly.

Bitter Creek saw Jackson's arm jerk. He went for his own gun. Simultaneous with several thundering detonations, the front lights of the saloon went out. In the half-light from the rear, men could be seen scuttling in every direction. The odor of burnt powder permeated the saloon, a pungent stench.

Gene Rule and Jackson went down, crouching; whether hit or not was not clear. Hank Chiles faded speedily into the background of dusk. Bitter Creek staggered off, cursing. He had been shot somewhere. Even Billy lurched from the sting of a graze. Jess Catlin violently shouldered him toward the door.

"Leggo o' me!" Billy was wild. "What the hell kinda fightin' man am I s'posed to be? Them short-horns'll think they got me on the run! Damn you, Jess——" He choked back his agonized mortification.

Outside in the street Jess fell taciturn, letting go his grip on Billy. There was no indecision, however, in the way he steered a course toward their tethered ponies. In five minutes they were in the saddle and swinging the heads of the animals toward Lost Cabin Creek.

The Orpha was once more filled with laughing, talking groups as they rode past.

It had been late in the evening when they arrived at Fetterman, and was now past midnight. From the north-west the wind soughed drearily. In the black, starless sky, lightning played with humid continuity and thunder mumbled and muttered. Jess watched uneasily as they rode. He made no comment when the first large drop of rain splashed his cheek.

The storm came down with a swoop. The advance gust of the wind tore at them sharply. Rain slapped like shot and the horses shied. Almost at that moment the fury of the elements tore loose. Lightning lashed out, bombarding the prairie with a heavy cannonade. The deafening noise rolled along the open ground.

"This'll play hob with the steers!" Jess called anxiously above the uproar. "The boys'll keep 'em from tearin' loose, but they may drift clar to the Platte!" It was plain the prospect gave him no peace. In the lightning flashes Billy saw his face lifted to the sky in watchful study.

Without discussion they turned broadside to the blast and pressed on in a more southerly course. Their clothes, their ponies, streamed with pelting rain.

By nature of its violence the storm was of brief duration. When it had rumbled away south and the downpour slackened to a nagging drizzle, they rode on at a steady trot. Silence, except for the sloshing of the ponies, returned to enfold them. The darkness was profound.

It was a ride that continued for several hours, touched with grimness on the part of Jess. The tireless quality of concern for the cattle was again uppermost in him. Dawn light touched the east and revealed his face stern and rock-like. They rode out on the bank of the Platte and turned west to follow the river. Swelled with the contribution of local creeks, it swirled along dark and turbid.

There was no sign or sight of cattle, and as he gazed keenly the lines of Jess' face eased. Perhaps the Pitchfork herd had not drifted from the creek. Billy was on the point of suggesting that they swing in that direction when he saw Jess pull up to stare at the soggy ground.

"Hell's fire!"

Jess growled in his throat wrathfully. Billy pushed up beside him to peer. Clear and unmistakable, the path of a madly racing herd led down to the river's edge. The Pitchfork steers had not only left the grazing ground but were beyond the Platte!

Jess thrust his pony into the water without hesitation. His hawk-like gaze was trained on the farther bank. Beyond it the Laramie Mountains bulked faintly.

"How d'you know you ain't bargin' into quicksand right now?" Billy called after him exasperatedly.

"I don't! That's a chance I'm takin'!" Jess snapped over his shoulder. In another moment his mount was swimming strongly.

Muffling his curses, Billy plunged after. The ponies

fought the current valiantly. It was with no little effort that they won across and scrambled up the southern bank, blowing gustily and flirting the water from their steaming flanks.

Jess headed south. Scattered and wide-spread, the herd left a bewildering but unmistakable trail. They rode without let-up, the game cow ponies covering the ground in long leaps.

"There's a bunch!" Billy howled ten minutes later, pointing. "An' there's another!"

Jess had seen them. The sun was just touching the horizon with golden fire. A broad beam flashed down across the rain jeweled range to reveal at a distance many cattle—apparently the entire herd—spread out over a large area and grazing quietly.

"Something's quar about this!" Jess thought, frowning as he gazed. The dwarfed figures of riders here and there did not satisfy him. Together he and Billy drummed toward the herd.

"They been stopped some way, Jess!" the latter burst out, his own curiosity prodded. "No punchers ever pulled 'em up in that shape—all strung out!"

Jess was already occupied with the problem. A faint glint in the rosy sunlight, seen for an instant and then gone, seemed to afford him an incredible explanation. Still he spoke no word, his strong face portentous.

It was Billy who exploded with the discovery of the amazing truth. His eyes were narrowed to dangerous slits as he stared past the bunched and lowing cattle.

"Jess, them steers can't go no farther!" he cried

hoarsely. "They've piled slap dab up ag'in a bob-wire fence!"

The posts could be seen now. Jess' rock-hard gaze was already following the new, shining strands extending east and west across the range between two out-flung arms of the Laramie Mountains, as far as the eye could reach.

CHAPTER FOUR

SAN SABA SPEAKS

RAIL-STRAIGHT in the saddle, an early break-
fast under his belt and the zest of living in his
heart, San Saba Lee rode away from the tumbledown
old Tincup line camp at Dry Creek in the pearly dawn.
His plain but strong face expressed good-nature as he
dropped the reins over the battered horn and built
himself a morning smoke with slim, competent fingers.
His blue levis and cotton shirt were faded but clean.
His Stetson was tilted jauntily on the sorrel head. The
steady blue eyes were open, unclouded, keen.

His way led through sparse clumps of sage and
matted buffalo grass until he came to the fence that
marked the boundary of the range belonging to his
employer, Colonel Dickson Purdy. He swung the dun
pony and racked down the endless line of posts.

His eyes narrowed briefly as they encountered the
barb-wire. He had little use for it personally. It was
an innovation, every yard of it strung within the past
fortnight upon land which hitherto had known no semblance of a barrier, and this was the first time that he
had seen this particular fence. His gaze ran ahead
curiously as he rode. It was just possible that the storm
had driven stray stock down from the north against
the fence.

"If that was to happen, the ownehs might drift along after it," he mused to himself; "and when they see bob-wire, it bein' something of a shock, they might begin to pull hair. And afteh that they're just as likely to begin pullin' fence wire. . . . The Kunnel wouldn't want that, an' I reckon I don't either."

It was an example of the kind of thinking that had made him, two weeks ago, and only a few days after he had gone to work for Colonel Purdy, the foreman of the latter's extensive and prosperous Tincup Ranch.

Five miles below Dry Creek he came within sight of scattered cattle along the north side of the fence. A handful had broken through and were moving on this side of the wire. He rode forward without haste or hesitation, his thin-lipped scrutiny picking out several horsemen amidst the outspread steers.

The J B brand on the nearest cow told San Saba nothing. Even at a distance, however, he noted a variance in ear-marks. He frowned slightly when he came close enough to read the Pitchfork brand on the majority of the long-horns.

"Jess Catlin's herd," he murmured, his eyes slanting back quickly to the riders. A picture of Rhoda Catlin's face arose unbidden before his thoughts.

The members of the little group had spied San Saba and were gazing toward him. After some low-spoken words, one of them swung his pony and advanced. A glance showed him to be an elderly and bearded stranger.

"Whut's the meanin' of this?" he called stridently,

waving his hand toward the fence. "Is that the way you're treatin' other cowmen down hyar now?"

San Saba examined him intently without speaking. His face was expressionless as he approached the fence and drew up, to gaze past the man at his companions. Glen Catlin sat his bay with sober mien. Rhoda, on foot, looked across her pony's back with unreadable eyes.

"Good mornin', Glen. Howdy, ma'am," San Saba greeted easily. He had known them long before he got his present job.

"Howdy, Lee."

Glen touched his horse and rode forward. Rhoda walked at his side, the reins of her pony in her hand. Her hips were slim as a boy's in the loose overalls. Her stride was smooth and unhampered.

San Saba's features were grave as he met Glen's reserved inspection. "So it's Lee now?" he queried quietly.

The bearded man exploded in a disgusted snort. "Nemmind the frills, mister!" he broke in, breathing noisily. "Mind explainin' this hyar freeze-out fer us?"

San Saba looked at him again, closely. "Who is this man?" he asked Glen bluntly.

Glen told him, smiling slightly. Listening, San Saba took note of that smile. It meant that he had cracked through the cold surface of hostility. As she came close, he saw also that Rhoda's regard was not as cool as he had imagined it. Both she and her brother were splashed with mud, their clothing damp, their faces tired. Their lack of warmth was no doubt due, at least in part, to this.

San Saba nodded. "I expect yore stuff come quite a ways last night, if it got started good," he offered easily.

"We bedded down on Lost Cabin Creek——"

San Saba's brows rose. "Up north of the Platte? You did come a ways!" he exclaimed.

"Way to hell an' gone farther'n I expected—with this at the end!" Brush interjected with gruff heat.

San Saba's brows drew down. "You," he told Brush annoyedly and with directness, "talk too much."

Old Joe was so amazed that his jaw dropped.

Rhoda's eyes, when San Saba returned his attention to her, were quizzical. His liking for her low, rich voice left him aware that she had spoken no word as yet.

A quiet, almost a silent girl, she was in no wise inconsiderable. San Saba had met her perhaps half-a-dozen times in the past three years, once as far south as Baxter Springs, in Kansas, and had spent possibly two hours in her company altogether; yet he felt that he knew her well. She was one girl whose impulse seemed to him predictable according to common sense. This, and something else about her not so readily explainable, had kept her fresh and vital in his memory when the figures of other women were apt to fade with celerity.

"Why don't you-all ride oveh to Dry Creek, if you've a mind to?" he suggested, pointing out that although the barrier was up against the Catlin stock, the restriction must not be considered to include themselves. "There's grub oveh there, and water."

"But not a drop fer them steers this side o' the Platte!" Joe Brush persisted harshly. "Dammit man, it's not two mile to Feather Creek, over yore line! Why in nation did that fence have to go jest hyar?"

"Brush, the fence is there now. Perhaps you'd like to speak to Kunnel Dick about it," San Saba told him levelly. Pitched low, his voice was not without its note of warning.

It was so effective a check-mate that Brush could only scowl his baffled disgust.

"We won't get anywhere by arguin'," Glen Catlin put in shortly. "Might as well think about gettin' our cows together." Heeling his cayuse around as he spoke, he started for the steers which had passed through the hole in the fence made in their first wild dash against it. Red, the Shoshone, and Smoke Chaloner were already busy raking them out of the sagebrush. Grumbling loudly, old Joe swung his mount and followed.

Rhoda thrust her foot in the stirrup and rose to the saddle. Across the fence, San Saba waited for her. With the wire between them, they rode down toward the gap at a walk.

"Some of the cows are pretty well barked up," she observed, glancing critically at the legs and flanks crusted with dried blood.

"Ma'am, I'm right sorry you barged into this heah," San Saba declared earnestly.

She turned to regard him steadily with her calm

hazel eyes. "San Saba, do you approve of this?" she demanded flatly, indicating the wire.

He was honestly disturbed. "I can't say I don't approve of it," he pointed out. "It ain't heah for the trouble it would make."

"But you rather expected something of the sort?" she pressed on.

"Why, no!" he protested. "I hadn't a ghost of a notion——" He paused in the midst of an unnecessary lie. And yet there had been no thought of the Catlins in his mind when he started out. If their appearance signified trouble it was more than he would have seen in the arrival of another outfit.

"It looks as though you hadn't," Rhoda responded dryly, her glance dropping from the six-gun at his hip to the stock of the Winchester which protruded from his saddle-boot.

San Saba did not immediately answer. His face was oddly grim. In another minute they would come up with Glen Brush and the others, and his chance would be lost.

"It's ce'tainly a shame," he said hurriedly in a lowered tone, "that we should have to meet with this between us, afteh the winter." He flushed slightly and stole a glance at her. The first golden splash of the morning sun touched her hair with auburn, and he thought her beautiful.

Rhoda's faint, ineffable smile might mean anything. San Saba was not a little disgruntled with the present set-up. He would have to use all his tact to keep from antagonizing the entire Catlin outfit in the face of this barb-wire insult. The intemperate bluster of Joe Brush had given him an unexpected leverage on the sympathies of Glen Catlin, and perhaps on those of Rhoda. But there remained a far more difficult course to steer at the eventual appearance of Jess and Billy.

In the meantime, there was Brush to be dealt with. Joe was off his bronc, stamping flat the sagging strands of barb-wire. They would not lay down. He swore steadily in a monotonous chant of fury, and took a malicious pleasure in the flying staples which released the twanging wires from the posts that remained erect.

Several times San Saba and the others headed the stray steers for the opening in a bunch. When Brush stamped down the wire at one side of the gap, it sprang up on the other, or in the middle. The steers shied, with the perverse intent to forage deep into Tincup territory. Brush paid no attention to Glen's exasperated protests. He persisted in meddling with the wire, doggedly cursing the stuff. Conscious of deliberate badgering, San Saba exploded.

"Damn you, Brush—come out of theah, so's we can do something!" he snapped.

"S'pose you git afoot an' teach this hyah hell's red tape to lay down then!" Joe bawled.

San Saba was on the ground in a flash.

"Maybe it'd help if I taught you to do some layin' down!" he retorted.

Brush stumbled backward in ludicrous caution. "You wouldn' be so fat an' sassy if I'd brought a gun with me, ol' settler!" he snarled vindictively. "You think yo're the big buffalo bull around hyah, but I'll crawl yore hump yet!"

Hard-faced, San Saba volunteered no more as Brush pulled himself into the saddle, breathing fire. He knew the man represented the typical outraged cattleman's attitude toward the fence he was bound to support and protect. He could do no more than quell the other's resentful trouble-making.

A noncommittal witness of the incident, Rhoda noted with some amusement that old Joe's activities thereafter kept him at some distance from the offending barb-wire.

San Saba's brief truculence brought no weight to bear against her approval of the man. She still remembered the first time she had met him. He had helped her straighten out the entangled camp wagon at a mud-swamped bog, displaying the qualities which she had since found other cause to admire in him. His pleasing drawl had announced that he was from Texas, although the incident in question had taken place in south-eastern Colorado.

His dark-red hair and smiling eyes, together with an uncommon ease and grace of body, had made him an object of unusual interest to her. She was therefore not displeased when he found occasion later to murmur to her: "I'm ce'tainly sorry this had to happen, ma'am. I'll be looking to hunt you folks up when the air is clearer."

There was no opportunity for answer. At that moment, hearing the imperative pound of hoofs, both glanced up to see Jess and Billy Catlin bearing down on them with harsh, intent faces. Caught unawares, San Saba turned to meet his real problem.

Glen had seen his brothers also. He came through the gap in the fence, behind the last of the strays, to join the converging group. Joe Brush was close behind him.

CHAPTER FIVE

JESS SHAKES HIS HEAD

"BOB-WIRE!" cried Billy Catlin like a bitter curse, pulling his pony to a slithering stop. "San Saba, whut in hell've you got to do with this?"

"I've got to ride around inside of it," the Tincup foreman responded ruefully. His gaze, however, was all for Jess as the latter got down heavily.

"Lee, I've heard about these big spreads an' thar doin's. Now I'm seein' it! Whut's yore stand on all this?" Jess demanded. He was primed for bear.

"You know whut his stand is!" Joe Brush threw in hoarsely. "To hell with us!" His small, predatory eyes glinted over the hawk-beaked nose.

He did not get down from his saddle, nor did Billy. All the others were on their feet. Glen, Rhoda and Smoke Chaloner stood a little apart, listening and alert. Even Red had ridden in and dismounted, his dark visage unmoved.

Jess was boring San Saba with opaque, flinty gaze. "Are you standin' in with the big fellers—throwin' us down?" he went on with bull-like care.

"I'm workin' fo' the Tincup, Jess," San Saba answered gently. "Maybe if you'd say what we've been doin' to you . . ."

Jess was ponderous. "This fence," he began, his

frown darkening as he glanced at it. "Mebbe you don't wanna say why it's thar, Lee."

"Sho'! That's easy. . . . It's to keep Kunnel Dick's cows in, Jess, and others out," San Saba explained persuasively. "Look: it's done saved you trouble already. The storm starts yore cows, and the fence stops 'em. You couldn't ask no more of a fence you'd built yoreself, Jess."

A smile appeared momentarily on Rhoda's face.

"Why'd Purdy put up this hyar fence, Lee?" her brother demanded bluntly.

San Saba dissembled his confusion. He had been asking himself that question. "Kunnel Dick didn't confide in me," he pointed out simply.

"Was it because this valley is the straight trail through the Lar'mie Mount'ns to Medicine Bow from the north?"

"No," said San Saba succinctly.

"Good Goddle mighty!" Joe Brush exploded wrathfully. "D' you have to know why he built it, Catlin?"

Jess' peremptory stare silenced the bearded buffalo hunter.

"Purdy claims a good half of this hyar valley. The Spade outfit seems to've staked out the rest," the former went on bitingly. "C'n you say whether they've fenced in too, Lee?" He accompanied this with a sharp scrutiny.

"Reckon I did heah they'd done something of that kind," San Saba admitted.

"Hell's hinges!"

Billy's cayuse jumped under the raking spur, and then trembled, stamping, as he jerked it down. "You heard!" he snarled. "The hull valley blocked off, eh? An' we're s'posed to put up with that? Why, damn yore gall, feller——!"

He jerked the horse around savagely, fumbling with his coiled rope. His face was murderous.

"Billy!" Rhoda exclaimed indignantly.

"I'll put a hole in that fence a mile wide!" Billy burst out bitterly. "An' that goes fer the next one I meet too!"

"I wouldn't do it, Billy, if I was you," San Saba told him levelly. His face was pale.

"Who ast you if you would or not?" Billy flamed at him. ". . . Git on yore hoss, Jess, an' we'll settle this pronto!"

"Billy, come down off the peck an' be a man!" Glen Catlin called ringingly, taking a step forward. "If you've got to bust a cinch, take it out on yoreself, you hothead! . . . San Saba's come out here alone to face us, an' no fuss about it; but you can't see that!" He swung back to Jess. "Now go to it, an' talk it out! Puttin' on war paint won't get none of us no more cows—or more range either!"

Billy flung down his hat, cursing, and slid off his pony to stamp angrily away.

San Saba flashed Glen an appreciative glance. If his watchers wondered at his evenness of temper it was because they did not realize the importance of the stake for which he played. Rhoda's hand came down from her throat, and Smoke Chaloner shifted his feet more easily.

Jess, however, remained undecided, his gaze keen in his craggy face.

"I don' know how to figure you, Lee. You say one thing, but yore boss's actions say another!" he declared sternly. ". . . Fence clar from one side of these hills to the other! Why man, I've drove steers down through hyar before you ever saw the country! Can you gimme one good reason why that wire should stay thar?"

"I reckon because Kunnel Dick says it should, Jess," replied San Saba evenly. "He's proved up on this land, or had it proved. It's his, an' he can do what he wants with it."

Jess' featured reddened. "I dunno's he kin," he denied. "Whar's that leave the man that's drivin' through? It's two hundred miles an' more through the Lar'mies ary other way!"

"But you ain't goin' south now, Jess," San Saba argued. "I'm just done tellin' you this heah fence saved you trouble this mornin'."

"It ain't now, an' it ain't only this hyar fence, I'm hot about!" Jess contradicted hardily. "It's ary time an' ary fence! It's the confounded idee of the thing! I tell you this terr'tory's allus been free-range, an' it allus will be"

"No it won't, Jess." San Saba shook his head decidedly. "Yo're all wrong about——"

"I tell you it will!" Jess almost shouted. He was

beginning to breathe fire. "We'll keep this range clar if we have to haul down ever' fence we come to!"

"Well, maybe I didn't say it just right," San Saba conceded patiently. "I ain't tryin' to get you riled, Jess."

"You don't have to try. Lee, I've knowed you for two-three seasons now, an' you struck me as bein' pret' near white. This is the fust time I've known you to back a blazer like this hyar! Whut in tarnation hell's got into you, man? Yo're a cowman! You know whut's right an' whut ain't!"

"Why, if you put it that way, I can see points to yore argument, Jess," San Saba answered feelingly. "I've knowed you a while too—I don't have to say that I've he'ped you along a time or two," he added deprecatorily; "but that goes to show what I think of you. Why don't you come over to the ranch with me and have a talk with Kunnel Dick? I'm sho' he'd make you see——"

"I won't stir a stump past that wire. The sun'll never set on the day I've rode around inside a fence in Wyomin'!" The pulse in Jess' forehead beat thickly. "An' whut's more, I don't want no truck with Purdy! How c'n he explain blockin' off a trail I've drove over afore he come out of Tenn'see?" Scorn and rejection rang in the words.

"Now, Jess, yo're all hot about this heah. When you come to think it over——"

"I don't half to think it over! I'll be figurin' to do somethin' about it next!" Jess snapped.

"—it'll look altogether different," San Saba went on without batting an eye. "I know mo' men than I can count on my two hands that say Jess Catlin is the squarest shooter in the cattle game. A week ago I said to myse'f I could count on you to understand my position. I thought, Catlin, he'll savvy the play, and stay by me. And Jess, I'm still hopin'."

His cajolery was not without effect. Jess' choler subsided to reluctance. He looked down and away, striving to marshal the scattered forces of his grim position.

"That's all right fur's it goes, San Saba," he countered in an altered tone. "But it don't change things a bit. Whut's nice is one thing, an' whut's fair is another! Whut I want is fer you to give me reasons fer backin' off. You can't!"

"Why, I can try," said San Saba. ". . . I expect you know what the winter did to a lot of cowmen, Jess?"

The latter jerked a nod.

"Sho'! It got pretty deep into us—an' I bet it got to you too. Eh?" San Saba's tone was conversational now. "Still we was lucky. Lots of fellers got wiped out —with no grass showin' above the ice, an' the stock dyin' like flies an' all."

"Still, I don't see——" Jess began.

"Yes you do!" the other urged. "Jess, you cain't make money on trashy stuff—runts and stringy wild steers and so on. So Kunnel Dick figures to breed up the strain. Better stuff—more money. You can see that.

Gives the boys steadier work too. No more winter lay-offs."

"Don't go gittin' away from the point now, San Saba!"

"Wait. You got to look after high-grade steers, ain't you? Got to feed 'em maybe, in winter, an' keep an eye on 'em. You cain't be tailin' 'em up a hundred mile down-trail so's they'll stand up to the hay wagon. An' so you build a drift-fence——"

Glen and Rhoda were listening intently; Smoke Chaloner, as a stern product of the old order, rather more sceptically. Jess rubbed his jaw, glancing keenly. He paid no attention to the louder grumbles of Billy and Joe Brush, a little apart, and wholly contemptuous.

"And what's more," San Saba went on spinning his web, "you ain't goin' to have bred-up stock long if it mixes in the brush with just ev'thing that comes along. It's like folks runnin' with their kind—but shucks, you never could get a cow to show taste!" He grinned briefly. An answering crevice crossed the features of Red, the Shoshone, to whom San Saba had tactfully addressed the remark.

"So there's yore fence, Jess—reason and all," the latter concluded easily. "In ten years it'll be accepted ev'where in the territory. You'll be buyin' spindles of the stuff yorese'f in five! It protects you and it protects the other feller. I told you it cuts both ways, an' yo're feelin' the wrong aige now—but you'll see! I'm talkin' straight!"

But he was going too fast for Jess, who was not going to be so readily crowded past the usurpation of his range rights. They discussed the matter pro and con, with varying degrees of heat. From time to time Glen put in a pertinent word, and Smoke Chaloner was provoked to an occasional gruff ejaculation.

They got nowhere with the inevitable deadlock. When Jess finally withdrew from the contest it was upon the frank note of hostility in abeyance.

"Don't think I'm satisfied with this the way it stands, San Saba, because I ain't!" he summed up gruffly, pulling his lanky frame into the saddle. "You've talked me into a sack, but you can't do that with a couple thousan' steers! You better put on a session with Purdy an' make him see the error of his ways—or else git yoreself another job!"

He turned to the others, footing their stirrups as they made ready to move. His voice rose: "We'll bunch the stuff afore we head fer the Platte. You, Billy—an' Smoke—make a swing round the flank thar, an' git 'em movin'." He swung his arm.

Billy's face was bitter as he started to comply. The smouldering look in his eyes promised the Tincup foreman that matters had not been concluded to his liking, but that there would be another day. Joe Brush also favored Lee with a wolfish regard. Rhoda's grave, understanding gaze, as she turned away, was all the sympathy San Saba was to receive. She realized fully what he had been up against.

The long-horns bawled as they were rounded up and

started north for the river. Working in unison, the riders accomplished their task with dispatch.

Watching them ride away, San Saba unconsciously sighed his relief. "That was no snap," he murmured, as he recalled how narrowly he had averted a clash. "No use worryin' though. Sho' plenty of time for that. Other folks'll be along, I expect, and I'll have it to do all over again—if I can. Right now I reckon I better fix this heah hole."

His brows knit as he set about straightening the entangled strands. There could be no doubt that the fence would be the cause of serious trouble within the next few weeks.

He was amazed at the position in which he found himself. A month ago he had been a carefree cowboy who had never laid eyes on barb-wire. On the payroll of a Texas ranch—that of an uncle—with the first days of the southern spring he had joined a trail drive covering sinuous miles and carefree weeks, until, once in Wyoming, a bewildering succession of events occurred which had altered the course of his life.

Reaching its destination near Fetterman, the herd had been sold and its respectable purchase price handed over to the Texas trail boss. Then, in one night at the wild frontier town, this man—old "Cap and Ball" Lee's trusted employee—had gambled away most of the money. Learning what was afoot, San Saba charged the man with his defection and precipitated a furious fight from which he emerged beaten and bested.

The trail boss and his henchmen made good their escape.

It had been a severe blow to San Saba. Knowing his uncle's dour character, he had not ventured to return to Texas with the bitter truth, choosing rather to take the responsibility of reparation on his own shoulders. It was for this reason—to repay the stolen money for the Texas herd—that he had sought his present position, facing courageously the atonement of another man's crime.

There were times when his situation lay heavily on him. He told himself no man need take the course which he had chosen. But he did not relinquish his object, knowing what the trail herd had meant to his aging uncle. Remembrance of this strengthened his resolve and made his resentment burn against the man who had brought about such a state of affairs. It left him grimly content to remain in Wyoming, awaiting the day when he should meet the trail boss face to face, and force an accounting.

Gazing after the diminishing form of Rhoda Catlin as he reflected on these things, San Saba shook his head slightly. "I'd feel plenty betteh, knowin' she was out of this," he mused bleakly. There was little assurance in the remembered charm of her quiet eyes that her presence would add to his peace of mind in the days to follow.

CHAPTER SIX

TOO MUCH TO TAKE

FOLLOWING the bawling herd with a moody face, Jess Catlin reviewed stolidly the results of his wrangle with San Saba Lee. To his perplexed disgust he could find nothing whatever favorable to himself. San Saba had used only quiet, conciliating talk calculated to smooth over the turbulence of his protest. And it had worked.

"Damn him, anyway!" Jess muttered discontentedly. "He's the first man I've let soft-soap me in many a month! Why'd I do that, now?" There was an element of wrathful wonderment in his tone.

San Saba had had him at a disadvantage. He had made Jess give over something for which he had the most serious concern, in exchange for a confidence which he resented. Gazing away unseeing to the hazed brown Laramies in the west, his jaw clamping, the latter gave way to slowly reviving ire.

"Wal—that's a game that'll work jest once, with me!" he promised grimly. But it was all he could do to wether the blow to his pride that it had worked at all. His self-disgust presaged rocky going for San Saba the next time they met.

The shortness of Billy and Joe Brush with him did nothing to improve his temper.

"If you'd only give the word to go after that wire, while we had the chance!" Billy's accusative ejaculation sounded above the rumbling ground murmur of hoofs. "But no, you had to play big with that blame foreman! What does he mean to you? . . . Now we've jest walked away from the deal!"

"Nemmind, now!" Jess lashed back at him savagely, his face like granite. "We ain't done with this by a long shot! This hyar is free land, an' nobody can change that!"

"San Saba an' his boss're makin' a pass at changin' it too damn fast to suit me!" Billy flung back flatly.

Glen rode close and peered at his brothers watchfully. "Lay off, Billy!" he admonished. "You spoke yore piece an' it didn't come off. Let it go at that!"

"You pull yore horns outa this!" Jess told him with surcharged directness. "I give San Saba a chance to have his say, an' it didn't go down with me!"

"An' so whut're you goin' to do—talk about it?" Billy snarled brutally.

Glen began to curse his exasperation in scorching terms. "I suppose *you'd* like to go back an' shoot San Saba!" he ended bitterly.

"It'd gimme one hell of a lot of satisfaction!" Billy bawled back. "An' mebbe it'd give Dick Purdy somethin' to think about besides the price of short-horn, blue-ribbon steers!"

"No question about it!" Glen retorted contemptuously. "Trouble with you, Bill, you'd rather fight this out than settle it any other way!"

Joe Brush, riding on the other side of Billy, listened with feral expression. He appeared to have learned new caution during the morning, however, and kept his own counsel. Jess rode with his stern gaze straight before him, fumbling the impassé with habitual slow certainty.

"You c'n both fergit about it!" he put in decisively. "I'm tellin' you hyar an' now I've took cards in this game. If I figure to play 'em close to my vest, that's my business!" There was no mistaking the authority in that tone.

"Wal, hell's blue blazes! I'll shore be tickled to see you stop throwin' away aces!" Billy rowelled him wickedly.

Jess blew up volcanically, rumbling like a hurt grizzly. His weathered cheeks were the color of red-hot copper.

"I've told you afore, feller—if you don't like the way I do things, you c'n roll yore war-bag any time!" he rumbled. "In the meantime, you c'n pull yore stake an' hit fer Fetterman. Git hold of Hank Chiles an' anybody else we know, an' bring 'em out to the Platte. Tell 'em I'm wantin' to powwow—an' don't take no fer an answer! That'll give you somethin' to do, you Injun!"

Billy was white to the lips, his eyes flashing. He did not demur. Watching him with the shrewd distrust of experience, Glen saw the subtle blaze of intention in his face.

"Don't send him to Fetterman, Jess!" he protested. "That's jest exactly what he wants!"

"You wouldn' let me have what I want if you could help it, would you?" Billy snapped at him cynically.

Glen jerked the bridle impatiently and turned off to flank the lagging herd. He was done with the discussion.

Joe Brush spoke up gruffly in the ensuing silence: "I'll go 'long with Billy, Catlin, if yo'll watch my critters. Chiles an' them fellers'll listen to me!"

Jess vouchsafed no rejoinder beyond a noncommittal grunt. In another moment, Billy and old Joe pulled away from the herd and struck out across the plain for the Boxelder crossing of the Platte.

Watching them go, Rhoda was filled with misgivings. Following her hard-learned custom of trust in Jess, however, she made no allusion to the matter, contenting herself with flashing a smile of consolation at Glen.

As they drew apart, Billy and Joe Brush fell into animated and sulphurous agreement on the status of affairs.

"Damned if I see why he's so slow an' cautious!" the latter burst out harshly, referring to Jess. "By Godfrey, if it'd been me——"

"You don't know Jess," Billy interrupted bluntly. "He's slow, shore—but brother, he's hard too! When he hooks two an' two together you'll see fur fly! Once you git Jess started, he's hell on wheels! Wait'll we see Chiles. He'll put a bee in Jess' ear, or I'm a Chinaman. It won't take no spade bit to start *him* sunfishin'!"

he concluded contemptuously, his hard face set toward Fetterman and action.

They were to meet Chiles sooner than they expected. Half-a-dozen miles from the Pitchfork herd, his eyes restless and keen, Billy pulled into stare at a low, hovering dust pall which crawled along the melting brown prairie far to the east.

"Trail herd!" he muttered briefly. "An' travelin' south!"

"Wal, now!" old Joe concurred cheerfully. "That's somethin' like! . . . Whar you goin'?" he broke off, as Billy started in the new direction.

"Where d'you think?" the latter flung over his shoulder. His manner became intent. "I'm goin' to see who that is, an' find out if a lil' discouragement'll make him take water!"

Together they pushed their ponies toward the distant herd.

"Must be two-three thousan' in that bunch!" Brush ejaculated, when they had come close enough to see. "Three, four—thar's five men with it, anyway! Six!"

Two riders on the flank of the herd had discovered their approach. Their faces were turned, but they rode on, almost side by side. Neither raised a hand. When Billy and Brush drew near enough for identification, however, it was another story. One of the trail drivers was Hank Chiles. He turned his bronc out to join them.

"Wal! Thought you was a couple other fellers!" he greeted, a smile easing his taut gills. His eyes were slitted against the lurid sunlight. "Whut you doin' out hyar?"

Billy ignored the query. "Whut're you doin', Hank?" he countered keenly. "Where you headin' fer?" He had already noted the brand on the steers, a Rocking R—not Chiles' brand.

Hank's face fell. "Aw—— My bunch took a push in that storm, an' I'm lookin' fer it! . . . No harm done, I guess—Blue's with the steers. But Catlin, they're likely strewed all over Spade range right now—an' I tole you last night whut Mackey thinks o' that!" He grinned briefly. "I come up with Bandy Packer, here—" he waved a hand —"an' seein' Pack's trailin' south, I j'ined up."

Gazing at Packer, Billy seemed moved by some inward pressure, his eyes glinting.

"Man, yo're sittin' in with a straight flush, an' no mistake!" he exploded forcefully. "D'you *know* what yo're headin' for?"

Bandy Packer grinned wolfishly. He was a small, gnarled man of indeterminable age and leathery features. "I guess I'll come out on the other side!" he responded dryly.

"On the other side of what?" Billy jerked out. "That's the nubbin! . . . Pack—Chiles—in five miles yo're comin' plumb up ag'in bob-wire! Did you know that?"

The two men were profanely amazed. "Bob-wire!" "Catlin, are you lyin' to us?" they flung at him.

Billy's visage was like iron. "You know how to find the answer to that!"

Chiles and Packer mauled the situation with profane thoroughness. Colonel Purdy's turpitude was aired and digested. Approaching riders were hailed forward and given the amazing news. Bitter Creek winked at Billy and twitted his employer. The prospect of a range war did not feaze him. Chiles, on the other hand, could not get over it.

"Man, I was on the Boxelder a week ago! They wan't a smell o' bob-wire thar then!"

One rider who racked forward from the rear was not accosted. It was "Dogsoldier" Olsen, Billy saw with surprise—a rider for Colonel Purdy's Tincup spread. San Saba Lee's right-hand man, and the friend of every puncher on the range, the Swede was suddenly looked upon as the potential spy of the big stockmen. In the few minutes since the existence of Colonel Purdy's fence had leaked out, the air around the trail-herd had cooled considerably for him.

"Whut're you doin' here, Olsen?" Billy demanded shortly.

"Ay ban ridin' home, Catlin," Dogsoldier answered engagingly. "Ay vent to town to soak up a little nose-paint, yah!"

Billy hesitated, but said no more as the Swede passed on.

"He'll fade when he hears whut we say to 'is friends yonder!" Packer averred belligerently, winding up with a string of epithets. Nothing could now deter his march on the Spade range. Nor had the others any hesitation. Faces were turned forward in grim decision; mouths hardened.

"Bob-wire!" Packer snorted for the third time in as many minutes. "Why, that means they don't figure to let me trail acrost thar at all! We'll see about this, damn pronto!"

They had proceeded little more than a mile, the trail dust rising against the sky like a guidon of battle, when they descried a rider bearing down on them at a gallop. Packer, Billy, Chiles and others pressed forward.

"It's Old Blue!" Chiles exclaimed gruffly, recognizing his puncher's mount.

"Man, he's hurt too!" Bitter Creek seconded. "Lookit him huggin' the leather!"

Old Blue's cayuse thundered close and drew in. The puncher pulled himself erect and stared at them with smoking eyes. Blood soaked his tattered shoulder and his right arm hung limp. His hat was gone.

"Blue, whut in hell've you been up against?" Chiles called hoarsely.

"Plenty!" Old Blue fumed. "Hank—half the Spade outfit's over thar stringin' fence! They lit into me like a run of buffalo! They plugged three-four of yore steers that busted into the fence—an' when I yowled, they let fly at me with rifles! I was holed up fer a couple hours in a wallow, till the steers drifted in b'tween. Then I rolled my hump outa thar!" He wavered in the saddle, staring at the immense herd of onflowing cattle, and then at the fixed, wrathful faces of the accompanying men. "What're you aimin' to do? Whar you goin'?" he demanded.

"Hell's fire, man! What d'you expect? . . . we're goin' over thar an' bust through that fence akitin'!" It'll be jest too bad fer anybody that gits in between!"

Growling his gratified amazement, Old Blue swung in abreast. Wounded as he was, he would not cry quits, despite the urging of the others that he ride on to Fetterman for treatment.

"This jist suits me!" he asseverated with a comical and blood-thirsty leer. "Them Spade fellers've got it comin', no two ways about it! I'm bunged up jist 'nough to put me into the discard, but I'd like to see ary son-of-a-buffalo git b'tween me an' my chance of watchin' it!"

CHAPTER SEVEN

THE END OF HIS PICKET-ROPE

IT was early afternoon when the Spade range fence hove in view across the shining prairie. Marked by the scattered mass of Hank Chiles' cattle, it was presently identified as the ardent sun glinted in thin silver lines on the bright new strands.

Chiles cursed at the sight of his grazing steers. Bandy Packer stared ahead with narrowed lids, from which the cross-hatched lines ran down his cheeks to the knotted mahogany jaws. It was Packer who gruffly pointed out the presence of several men beyond the wire.

"Where?" Bitter Creek demanded, gazing.

"Right behind Hank's cows, there," answered Packer. He pointed them out.

No one said anything further as they rode on. All eyes were trained ahead unwaveringly. Conscious of generalship, Bandy Packer pondered his course of action.

"Hank," he said presently, "you an' me—Catlin—an' Brush here, 're ridin' ahead. We'll rip a hole in that fence. The rest of the boys stay with the bunch. Bitter Crick an' Blue'll turn the steers jest enough to miss Hank's herd. Cheyenne," he directed one of his own men, "ride back an' tell Bain what's doin'. An' when you see that hole in front of the herd, push 'em hard!" His instructions were clipped and crisp.

Cheyenne turned his pony and jogged away toward the drag.

Billy Catlin and Joe Brush spurred ahead, Hank Chiles following. Packer was more deliberate. He sat straight and firm in the saddle, his blunt face pugnacious. No one paid any heed to the huge Swede, trailing along in the rear.

The latter gazed away over the brown billows of the prairie to where they melted into obscurity along the heat-hazed horizon, or merged with the blue swell of distant hills. Conscious of brooding peace, Olsen was struck with the ironic pettiness of the conflict of men in such a land. He had no thought of attempting to avert it. He knew better.

He was fully aware that strife impended. Across Chiles' motionless herd he saw the alert heads of three men, their faces turned this way.

" 'Rapahoe's boys ban got somet'ing to tank about now, Ay guess," Dogsoldier mused, nodding to himself.

None of them returned to their pretended work as Packer's band trotted forward. When they observed the newcomers swinging toward the fence at one side of the grazing stock, they began to move along it to a point at which their paths would intersect.

The groups met over the barb-wire. There was no pretense of greeting, no unnecessary word. The thing that was boiling up in these men was action.

Billy Catlin, Brush, and Chiles drew up and stared.

Bandy Packer rode along the fence from one post to the next, peering sharply.

The three Spade men were drawn a little apart for freedom of movement. Their faces were set in stony opposition. The one mounted man, Gene Rule, carried a rifle. Denny Jackson and Arapahoe Jones, the two on foot, bore holstered six-guns. Jones was the foreman of the Spade outfit. His suspicious eyes followed the business-like maneuvers of Bandy.

"What're you aimin' to do, Pack?" he demanded finally, raising his voice.

Packer's glance bored into him. "I'm fixin' to find the loose ends, hyar. Failin' that, I'm goin' to bust plumb through, 'Rapahoe, an' you c'n do your own patchin'!"

"You ain't comin' through this line, Packer!" Arapahoe stated on a note of rising anger.

Bandy swung around. "That's yore mistake! We're comin' through, an' right now!" He flicked a commanding look at Hank Chiles. "Limber that rope o' yores, Hank. Might's well hook it on hyar anywheres!"

"Hold on!"

Arapahoe's hand was on his holster, the fingers rubbing uneasily. Denny Jackson was engaged in a similar occupation. "Don't you lay a hand on that wire, feller! I'm warnin' you!" Jones snapped.

Guns appeared in the grasp of Billy Catlin and Chiles, covering the Spade men. Rule, on his horse, likewise snatched at his hip. A spurt of flame jetted from Billy's side, the shot sounding flat and light in the immensity of space. Gene Rule cursed and his gun clattered. His bronc jerked, snorting, and then came to a trembling stand. The cowboy wrung his stinging fingers, turning a face of rage and hatred across the fence.

"Whoa!" Arapahoe Jones roared, his features wreathed in lines of towering anger.

A moment of tense truce followed. The lives of several men hung in the balance, so nearly at point-blank range were they.

"Damn you, Catlin!" Rule bawled his enraged bafflement. "I'll carve you loose from yore gizzard, yet, you——!" He added a string of sizzling epithets, at which Billy went white and cold.

"Wait, dammit!"

Bandy Packer took charge with a wrench, coming forward and presenting a face of thunder.

"Yore man had that comin' to 'im, 'Rapahoe—if yo're fixin' to make anythin' of it!" he barked. "But we ain't hyar for no shootin' match!" His searching glance took in every man within his range of vision. "Whut we are here for—in case yo're wonderin'—is to go acrost hyar, peaceful or otherwise! You c'n see my bunch acomin'." He waved a stocky arm. "When it gits here, there's goin' to be a hole waitin'!".

"Hang on, now, Packer!" Jones called, his hand up. "How d'you figure——"

"Git goin', you" Hank Chiles exploded.

"Shet up!"

"Dang you all fer a bunch of redskins!"

For a moment everyone had something to say, clamorous and heated.

"What're you doin' with this crowd of cutthroats, Olsen?" a voice demanded from the Spade side of the fence.

"Ay—Ay bane yust——" Dogsoldier began vaguely, looking his dumbest. He had made no move throughout the encounter, and had no pressing desire to be identified with either side.

The guns of Billy Catlin and Chiles were still trained across the fence. That of Denny Jackson had unconsciously drooped. Arapahoe Jones had lost his chance to throw down; while Gene Rule's opportunity to get at his rifle was non-existent.

"Let's get through here" Billy broke out intolerantly. "What're we waitin' for?"

The Packer herd was drawing nearer, accompanied by the hoots of the cowboys.

"Catlin——!" Jones exclaimed exasperatedly.

Bandy exhibited a smile of unfeeling resolve. "Do you gents mosey, or do you lay down hyar?" he ground out. "I've heard the ground stiffens a feller up," he added meaningly. His six-gun came out of the leather, glinting.

Arapahoe Jones swung away, cursing under his breath. "Let it go, boys!" he warned his companions.

They withdrew sullenly along the fence, muttering in low tones.

Hank Chiles put his rope on the barbed strands. Riding away, he tore the wire loose with loud, jangling snaps as the staples gave. Billy and Joe Brush snagged the second strand and wreaked a similar destruction.

An air of subtle triumph descended upon everyone. Dogsoldier Olsen had drifted off, ignored.

Sitting his saddle at the lip of the freshly-opened gap, Bandy Packer raised an arm in signal to the cowboys. The latter whooped, slapping with coiled ropes at their lagging charges. The first steers tossed their horns and came on. At the rear, the cattle ran a few steps as they were prodded, and then dropped back to their inevitable plod.

"What're they doin' over thar?" Chiles demanded of Billy Catlin, gazing after the departing Spade trio.

"Blamed if I know—or care!"

But Billy watched also. Arapahoe and his disgruntled men had paused, and Jones and Jackson were discussing something hurriedly. Billy saw the Spade foreman draw the rifle from Rule's saddle-boot, while Jackson pointed at the carcasses of several shot steers. Then Gene slapped the spurs to his pony and galloped off. Jackson, in the meantime, strolled to his own mount and procured a second rifle.

" 'Rapahoe an' Jackson're aimin' to hole up behind them dead cows!" Chiles burst out harshly. "We better root 'em outa thar! . . . Pack!" he called sharply to Bandy.

The latter had seen. "Why didn't we lay 'em out cold an' be done with it?" he snorted disgustedly. "Somebody'll have to work up through Hank's steers an' clear 'em out! An' watch out fer them rifles!"

But it was too late to avert threatening disaster. As the lead steer of Packer's herd pushed past the fence, Arapahoe Jones' rifle spoke. The steer stumbled, gurgling.

"God!" Bandy's face was writhing. He jerked the bridle ruthlessly. "Git out of hyar! He'll be cuttin' loose on us next!"

Jones' rifle spat again. A second steer went down. Within a minute the spiteful cracks had sounded a dozen times.

"What'll you do, Pack?" Billy Catlin cried hoarsely. "We can't stand fer that" His dark eyes were blazing with wrath.

"Wait, now!" Packer's manner was hard as flint. His gauging glance slanted about. Chiles, Brush, Bitter Creek and Cheyenne waited, their faces grim. Quickly Packer outlined his plan of action: "We'll work acrost the herd, an' go through the fence on the other side. Then we'll turn the bunch an' sashay up there! If them buzzards git tromped on, it's too bad!"

"But they're shootin' steers——!" Joe Brush began.

Packer jerked fiercely. "I don't give a damn about a dozen steers!" he ripped out. "Whut I want is to finish that skunk with the rifle!"

Chiles, Brush, Old Blue and Cheyenne began to work through the herd. There the swirling dust was as thick as a blanket, the heat suffocating. Billy Catlin pivoted his pony and, followed by Packer, raced at a dead heat around the flank of the press. Packer hailed Bitter Creek and Len Bain forward with them.

They met the others on the side of the herd away from Jones and Denny Jackson. Old Joe, Chiles, and the two cowboys seemed to have changed appearance in a few minutes. Their clothes were powdered white, their faces smeared and streaming with perspiration. Old Blue's lips were twisted with the constant pain of his throbbing shoulder.

"Listen, Pack!"

Above the clatter and bawling of the steers could be heard the continuing spang of the Spade rifles.

"Git past that fence, boys, an' start to turn 'em!" Packer's harsh voice held an edge of fury.

The rowelled ponies scampered ahead. In a moment they were on Spade land. Then slowly, relentlessly, with fiendish yowls and slapping ropes and hats, the men began to edge the massed steers to the right.

"Watch close!" Bandy warned sharply, in a yell. "Don't give them devils a chance at you! When you git a flash of 'em, throw down!"

Hounded and half-mad, the Rocking R cattle churned along the range fence in snorting confusion. The riders pressed forward amongst them.

It was Bitter Creek who discovered the flight of their quarry. His pony stumbled over the hulk of one of the shot steers. The cowboy pulled in with a jerk.

"Hank—Pack!" he roared. "They done skipped!"

The dust was thick, but Packer was as quick of perception as any. Through the choking murk the others heard his sulphurous outpouring of invective. Then his shadowy form appeared.

"Git outa this dust!" he bawled. "They can't be far! We'll spot 'em!"

They forced through the thinning steers. Then, from the edge of the boiling cloud, Hank Chiles raised a shout. The others wheeled in his direction.

Beyond the curtain of dust a slim, commanding man on horseback was pulled up, his face stern and critical. His presence bore a note of censure which somehow could not be ignored. Black eyes burned in the keen red visage.

Several yards behind him Gene Rule sat his panting bronc, a sullen expression on his graceless features.

"Wal, Mackey" Bandy Packer fumed, pushing to the fore. He had never met the resident manager of the Great Plains Cattle Co. but the militant bearing of the man, the open Norfolk jacket, the polished leather riding-boots, and the monogrammed HD brand on the pony told him all he needed to know.

Chris Mackey scanned the men drawn up before him. He did not know Packer, but a glimpse of Hank Chiles was sufficient for his quick mind.

"So you're back again," he addressed the latter flatly. His thin lips were habitually severe.

"Yo're damn right I'm back!" Hank burst out strongly.

The Spade manager waved this aside with a slim, hard hand. His glance narrowed as he snapped a look at the nearest cow. Then he was eyeing Packer again.

New to the western plains, Christopher Mackey was nevertheless something of an adept at meeting hard men. He regarded Bandy smoulderingly for some time in rankling silence.

It was Billy Catlin, restless and suspicious, who guessed what Mackey was waiting for. His searching scrutiny picked out the two cowboys some distance away along the fence to the east. At the same moment, Bitter Creek snorted from the other side of the group:

"There's 'Rapahoe an' Denny Jackson now, blast their hides!"

They were coming along the fringe of Packer's drifting herd from the south, their rifles across their saddle bows, their manner intent.

"You," Chris Mackey was saying measuredly to Packer, "talk too damned loud. Who or what you are—or what you do—doesn't concern me, until you overstep my rights." He let that sink in. "I don't have to tell you anything. But I will tell you that you don't belong where you are. And you've got to know I mean it!"

Packer's face was suffused with blood.

"Mackey, you needn't hide behind talk!" he bellowed domineeringly. "I won't ask you why this free range is closed! I know! It's yore damn bull-headedness, an' the mint of money behind you! I'm tellin' you yo're in wrong, an' you'll pay!"

It was Billy Catlin who saw the turn of the triumphant and retributive tide. Unless something was done about it Chris Mackey would prove a staunch, unpredictable rock against which Bandy's belligerence would beat to no avail. With a spurt of resolve, Billy thrust forward.

"Nemmind, beef-eater" he cut off Mackey's beginning acid rejoinder furiously. "We don't want no part of yore guff! What we want is action! Now, whut'll you do?" His goading defiance was murderous.

It was too late, however, to force the issue to advantage. The two Spade men, Colorado and Link Brazil, had swerved from the fence to reach Mackey and were now ranged beside Gene Rule. Arapahoe Jones and Jackson also came up, so that the Spade defense stood half-a-dozen strong.

"You don't have to shoot off yore mouth, Catlin!" Gene Rule thrust in now, vindictively. "We know yo're here!"

"We know yo're here too, Gene!" Bitter Creek retorted heatedly. He had not forgotten Rule's bitterness in the Orpha saloon, at Fetterman.

"Yes, an' if you wanto start the ball arollin'—begin!" Billy added contemptuously.

Gene Rule's visage was knotted with rage. "I'll see you in hell, Catlin, before I'll fight my picket-rope fer you!" he flamed. "You'd sell yore saddle fer my blood —but you won't git it!" His unconscious grasp on the rein made his pony rear, pawing. As it came down nervously, reacting to Gene's roiled passions, his hand streaked for his thigh and rose laden with compact, glittering death.

"Hey-ah-h!"

Billy's irresponsible howl rang weirdly. Immediately thereafter the two shots sounded as one.

Half the horses in the two groups whirled, surging. That of Billy Catlin flung its head, shuddering, and then collapsed, entangling Billy's leg as it went down. Gene Rule's bronc backed and wheeled, to break away from the spot at a hectic trot. Its rider, however, lay in a still heap between the prancing legs of the other ponies, where he had slid with a gasp, following the vicious crack of Billy's six-gun.

"Good Christ!" burst from Arapahoe Jones involuntarily. "You went an' killed 'im, you damned fool!"

Cursing frantically, his gun forgotten in his hand, Billy struggled to disengage his leg from the saddle-trappings and the weight of his dead pony. "Ya-as; an' I'll kill a few more o' you, soon's I tie loose from this blasted nag!" he flamed at Jones.

But his backing was fast fading away. The horses of the free-rangers whirled backward in threatened panic. Billy was left alone to face the enemy, pinned by one leg, and blinded by passion.

"I don't care if this is the end!" he raged insanely. "It'll be blame fast—an' in a blame good cause! Let loose yore wolf, you sneakin' devils! I'm ready!"

CHAPTER EIGHT

A DIFFERENCE OF OPINION

"A Y stick around dere yust long enough for the shootin' to commence," Dogsoldier Olsen grinned vaguely, "an' then Ay move off a lettle bit——"

"Shootin'!" exclaimed San Saba Lee softly, his face cast in lines of concern. "Dogsoldieh, are you sho' you wasn't mixed into that? What happened, man?"

They were in the doorway of the bunk house at Colonel Purdy's ranch, and the shades of evening were dropping slowly across the outspread range. The huge Swede had just ridden in and freed his grateful stallion in the pasture. His bridle outfit was still in his freckled hand.

"Ay ban talling you," he resumed patiently, his pale eyes alight. "It vasn't so bad as you tank, San Saba . . . When dose cows come t'rough the fence 'Rapahoe an' Denny knock down maybe ten-twalve. Then dem Spade men climb aboard an' pour outa dere.

"Bime-by dis Rule come up wit' Mackey. Cows spread all over dat place, an' the dust rollin' up! Packer's bunch come out of it—an' dere's the Englishman. Wal, dem fallers was all arguin' like hal, till Rule's pony blow up, an' come down—an' dere ban a couple shots, blam! Ay tank maybe——"

"Where was you, Dogsoldieh, when all this was goin' on?" San Saba put in shrewdly.

"He was busy blammin' outa there!" Pink Robinette put in humorously, from within bunk house.

"Why, as far away as Ay could get, San Saba, an' still be dere," Olsen responded innocently, ignoring the interruption of Pink. "Ay tank dose cows ban pretty goot cover, an' Ay sneak up maybe closer than Ay vant. But when the shootin'——"

"Well, hurry up, Dogsoldieh!" San Saba urged him on impatiently. "Let's heah what you saw, man! There was a couple shots, blam! An' then . . . ?"

Dogsoldier's bridle waved gently in his enormous hand; the only outward sign of irritation that he would permit himself. "Now, you look 'ere, San Saba! Ay vant to tell this in my own way, an' you——"

"Go on, then, Mist' Ericksen!" directed the Tincup foreman briefly. He was more intent on the other's story than he cared to reveal.

"My name ban Mister Olsen," said Dogsoldier with dignity. "Wal, Ay was in the cows when the shootin' began. Rule, he shoot—an' Catlin. Billy's bronc came down, an' Billy's leg under. He ban stuck goot, yah, an' fightin' crazy to get loose. Gene's pony run away fast; but not Gene. He ban stay put——"

"Shot!" exclaimed San Saba instantly. "Was he daid, Dogsoldieh?"

" 'Rapahoe, he yell that Billy ban kill him. Ay tank maybe so. Nobody stay to see. Dey get out of dere fast, yah! Pack—Billy—Chiles—dey talk fight planty.

But when the bang go off, Ay tank it scare 'em! . . .
'Rapahoe an' Denny an' Colorado haf the only rifles.
Brush, he ban got not'ing."

"And then what?" San Saba prompted, trying to
grasp the scene.

Dogsoldier's hand flapped. "Wal, dere was some
quick shootin'. Everybody movin' too fast to get hit.
Chris Mackey, he ban stand pat, mad an' cold inside—
Ay tank he look that way. But most everybody start
to move at first, San Saba, yah! Bandy Packer swing
his bronc, an' grab Billy by the arm. Billy ban come
loose, yellin' like an Injun; an' he pull on behind
Bandy, an' get away from dere, after the others."

"Them fello's? They all ran?" San Saba demanded
unbelievingly.

"No." Dogsoldier shook his head. "Bitter Creek, he
git mad, an' cuss, an' wave his gun. He ban all right!
Ay tank maybe he get shot. 'Rapahoe ban have his
rifle up. Dey stare at each other—Bitter Creek, an'
Chris Mackey, an' 'Rapahoe . . . Then Bitter Creek
yank his bridle an' ride away from dere, slow. He
look back an' cuss Mackey; then he look around an'
cuss Pack an' Hank an' dem fallers. Ay feel sorry for
him, yah. He ban licked by his own friends." Olsen
scratched his blond hair in the back. "Ay ban ashamed
for Chris Mackey," he confessed gustily. ". . . 'Rapahoe an' Denny ban watch the fence. The rest of dem
boys start pushin' Pack's steers back t'rough the hole.
Ay don't see . . ." Dogsoldier's kindly, little blue eyes
were narrowed, wandering away.

San Saba was not considering the ethics of Chris Mackey's stern course, however. He saw clearly now, in terms of results, what had happened at the Spade range fence that afternoon. For the first time in Wyoming history, to his knowledge, a southward-bound trail herd had been turned back, and protest successfully quelled. The first engagement in what he had no doubt was a dawning range war, had been decided. It might yet prove to be a costly victory for the large outfit. He knew to the last jot what it must mean to him.

"I reckon if I've got to steer a cou'se through this head business, I'd better find out where I *can* go," he mused. "I'll go have a confab with Kunnel Dick about it." He moved out of the doorway into the limpid light of the evening, and strolled up toward the house.

Colonel Dickson Purdy's ranch house was a sizeable structure of unpeeled white pine logs hauled down from the slopes of the Medicine Bow Mountains. Standing on a slight rise, it possessed a long gallery running along one side—a Wyoming bow, with appropriate reservations, to western Tennesseean antecedents—and was bowered with young cottonwoods, now a gray gauze against the pallid sky.

Approaching from the rear, where lay the outspread sheds, corrals, bunk house, blacksmith shop and the like, San Saba followed a beaten path around to the front. On the gallery he announced himself quietly to Miss Amantha Purdy, the Colonel's elderly, unmarried sister, and was let in to the comfortably appointed "library" immediately off the wide, house-high central hall.

The furnishings here were rough but adequate: rustic settles, over which were thrown gaudy blankets; a straight-back or two; the desk littered with journals and account books; deer and bear skins, on floor or wall; buffalo heads with darkly shining eyes, over mantel and door. On the "imported" library table were books and magazines, and a coal-oil lamp gave off a rich glow that spread over the room and the graying head of Colonel Dick, seated in a reading chair.

"Good evenin', San Saba. Take a chair, my boy."

Colonel Purdy did not rise, but his eyes lit up as he raised his head. He liked San Saba's serious face, his sensible conversation, and the air of vigorous youth he brought into the library. San Saba was just on the happy side of thirty.

"What've you brought to me tonight?" the older man smiled.

San Saba seated himself, his eyes grave: "It's that fence again, suh. I wish I didn't ever heah of fencewire."

"Well, I daresay there's worse things than ba'bedwire," Colonel Purdy said briskly, his hand restless on the chair arm.

"Maybe there is. I don't know what it can be," San Saba rejoined. He told in detail the results of his discussion with Joe Brush and the Catlins.

"Why, you came through that in excellent shape, and I'm proud of you," Colonel Dick pointed out, as though that settled it. Then he went on hastily: "Not that I agree with these fello's, San Saba! But there's bound to be a ce'tain amount of this until they've become educated."

"I'm thinkin' they maybe won't," the other went on quietly. "Kunnel Dick, heah's what happened this afte'noon." He related what Dogsoldier had reported of the violence at the Spade fence.

Colonel Purdy's faintly lined features were red and severe at the end. He was a tall, thin man with an ordinary benign countenance, and impeccable manners. Always a just man, he was nonetheless difficult to convince against his judgment.

"Beastly outrage! . . . Christopher Mackey is perhaps a thought over-determined," he went on candidly, "but there can be no question, San Saba, of the cou'se to be taken! Chiles' cattle accidentally broke Mackey's fence, and a hot-headed cowboy shot another in the shoulder. This Packer and his highbinders deliberately tore through the fence, and Christopher arrived in time to turn them back. And there's an end of it. They'll learn, these fello's!" he repeated his belief, shaking his head dogmatically. "It's no mo' than I would expect you to do for me."

San Saba perceived the difficulties of his position. "That's just it! Kunnel Dick, I wouldn't want to," he said firmly.

The Colonel looked at him in surprise: "Not want to?"

"No. You see, these small grazers are a plain lot,

Kunnel Dick; but they've got their rights. It was them, opened this head country—Catlin's folks, anyway."

"They opened it, seh—and then went away from it!" Colonel Dick interrupted.

"Why, don't you see, they opened it as free range, and they expect it to stay that way . . . This valley, Kunnel Dick, has been used fo' years by herds trailin' south to Medicine Bow. Until the railroads come in heah above us——"

"I don't see it!" Colonel Purdy gave away to slow heat. "Times have changed consid'able, San Saba, an' men'll change with 'em!" He knew this from experience. "Why, man——!"

"I ain't got down to my a'gument with you yet, Kunnel Dick."

The Colonel immediately melted. "I beg your pardon, my boy. You were saying——?"

"These small men." San Saba fixed his eye engagingly. "They're white, Kunnel Dick, if they're given a chance. They've done things fo' me. These Catlins turned back this mo'nin' on my say-so. They sho' deserve——"

"Talking to! Exactly!"

"You're not givin' me a chance. Not really," San Saba observed apologetically.

Colonel Purdy put on him a bright, searching look of inquiry.

"Maybe I should say you ain't givin' them a chance," the Tincup foreman went on. "It's ce'tainly the same thing. Kunnel Dick, if we refuse them an even break, they'll fight—they will so! They're on the peck right now, an' no mistake. It's somethin' to think about hard. There's many of them, and few of us. Kunnel Dick, shootin' in this country——"

"Oh, I know! Spunk, and vengeance, and a ce'tain amount of Damyank principle! It doesn't impress me!"

"Dead cows will impress you. Them—an' dead cowboys. And eve'lastin' fence repair!" San Saba was becoming short, his blue eyes stern.

Colonel Dick looked at him quickly. "San Saba, d'you think——?"

The latter's gaze was unbending. "A young war—that's what you and Christ'pher Mackey are invitin'! And you think that nothin' has got to be done!"

"Well, I'll change my mind." Colonel Purdy sat forward in his chair. "I'll get in touch with Mist' Mackey at once! We'll have to arrange fo' guards along that fence, and enough men to make ce'tain of our stand. Will you ride over to the Spade ranch in the mo'ning and tell Christopher I'll be with him tomorro' evening? By that time I'll have decided on my proper cou'se." The unfeeling executive was uppermost in him now.

San Saba got up and paced back and forth slowly. The Colonel's proposal embodied the most disastrous step he could have conceived. "I still think you're on the wrong track, suh," he said reluctantly.

"How so?" Colonel Purdy was doing his best not to bristle, and not succeeding at all.

San Saba sought a pacifying lead: "I don't think the Spade brand is the place to go."

"We differ!" the Colonel snapped indignantly.

"I know it, suh . . . Still I don't think so."

Colonel Dick made an exasperated gesture. "What do you think, then?"

"We should go straight to the little fello's—if you'll excuse me. Dicker with them and make them feel their impo'tance. You can't ignore them, Kunnel Dick! . . . I know how you feel about Chris Mackey: if you stand with him, you'll both be strong. Not so! You'll egg each otheh on—and you'll live on an island, enti'ely surrounded by enemies! Kunnel, suh, his way is wrong——"

"And yours is right?" the Colonel growled, his stern face flushed. They faced each other with tight lips and uncompromising eyes.

"Excuse me, suh," San Saba assented. "It is." He gazed at the floor for a moment before continuing: "Mackey's road is youhs, I know. I've reconciled myse'f to that. But if you could only go side by side, instead of hand-in-hand——"

The Colonel breathed stertorously in the succeeding silence. "It must be tremendously difficult for you to wo'k for me," he said stiffly.

It was San Saba's turn now to flush. "No, suh. I don't think it is." And then he added: "I told you I'd reconciled myse'f to it!"

"What!" Colonel Purdy's distended cheeks quivered. His tone was thunderous: "Young man, I've half a mind to——!"

"We sta'ted fightin' about the fence, suh," San Saba interposed desperately. "You can see how far we've got away from it."

Colonel Dick's stare was accusative. He began to prowl back and forth behind the table, his hands caught at his back. "I don't want to make up my mind too hastily. I will say that you've stepped oveh the bounds, Mist' Lee; and I don't intend to pass it by!" He pursued his dogged stride with knit, portentous forehead.

"Do you want this job you've got?" he fired out suddenly, stopping in his tracks.

"I—yes, suh," San Saba responded without hesitation.

"Ve'y well." Colonel Purdy was grimly decisive. "I'll figuah on that basis, while I think it ovah. In the meantime, you have youh instructions for tomorro'."

"I take it, suh, you are still determined to join forces with Chris Mackey?"

"San Saba——!" the Colonel began explosively.

"All right, suh!" the latter cut him off quickly. "I'll do as you say. I'm goin' now." Without reluctance he fired the Parthian shot which he had withheld for days: "Befo' I go, I want you to know how it looks. This mo'ning, Catlin asked me if you'd fenced because Mackey did. I said no—and I lied! Kunnel—suh—you built that fence in the first place because Mackey built one. You was afraid of how it would look, with two ranches side by side an' a fence around one of 'em! That is why I'm ashamed of it, suh! This country is not slow to see those things. Now you can judge for yourse'f!"

He walked toward the door as he spoke, and with a brief glance at his employer's apoplectic face, slipped through into the hall and closed the door softly behind him.

Silence reigned in the house, broken only by the faint jingle of his spurs as he let himself out upon the gallery.

"If that don't wind me up with him, nothing will," he thought moodly, as he walked toward the bunk house. "If Kunnel Dick th'ows his arms around Chris Mackey's neck, it won't be my doin's—tomorro', or any otheh time!"

He looked back at the glowing lights of the house half-guiltily. His self-admonitory murmur was sober: "It's plumb hell to have to th'ow down a fine old gentleman like him, even if it is fo' his own good!"

CHAPTER NINE

INJUSTICE TO ALL

R HODA CATLIN stuffed the latigo through the cinch-ring and yanked it home, regardless of the realistic grunts of her horse. Then straightening, she gazed absently across the saddle at the outspread long-horn herd in the middle distance.

The Pitchfork cattle had been returned to Lost Cabin Creek, and were quietly grazing. The morning sun gilded the scene brilliantly.

"I don't believe I like this country at all," she remarked sententiously to Glen.

Her brother glanced up from the leather quirt he was braiding, squatted on the ground. "Why not?" Behind him the camp wagon stood with open door and windows, hung along the eaves with kettles.

She waved an expressive hand. "Everything has gone wrong since we came, Glen. Everything. That fence, for an example. Joe Brush's wife bursting over here and ranting about her man! She feels it too, poor woman . . . Jess fretting and riding around, grumpy as a bear. Billy absolutely out of hand—Goodness knows where he is now! Somehow it seems——"

"Well, there're compensations, sis. San Saba Lee . . ." Glen glanced at her again, smiling.

No trace of pink showed in Rhoda's cheek, across

which a whisp of her brown hair blew. "I don't like it," she went on pensively. "That wire is unjust, and means trouble, I know. I suppose I shouldn't——" she broke off.

"You shouldn't——?" Glen prompted.

"Glen, when it comes to hot tempers, and promiscuous shooting . . . I think only of Jess, and Billy—and you!" she said hurriedly. "The way these men will go at things, nothing on earth can avert bloodshed!"

Glen jerked a rawhide strand taut, and shook his head. "Don't let your mind run on the thing like this, Rho. It's bound to take its course—turn out to suit itself. Don't you be worrying! You go on an' ride now. Everything'll be all right." A touch of impatience added realism to his tone.

Glen had long admired his sister's firm stoicism. As she swung into the saddle and cantered away with her head up, he found no reason to revise his opinion.

"She's dead game," he mused darkly, "an' she'll do her share of scrappin' when it comes. I wish she had a better break . . . It's a dang shame!"

Glancing back from a far swell of the prairie as she jogged along, Rhoda knew that he had tried to spare her for an hour from the weight of the inevitable. It had not worked. Ostensibly riding the country out of exuberance, as she so often did, she was really canvassing the possibilities of the future in solitude. She did not today see the broad, shining prairie, peaceful and endless and all-pervasive—but only the shadow hovering there.

"If only it had been another time!" she breathed, her heart contracting. "But now—Glen—Billy—Jess —San Saba!"

She could not deny her profound solicitude for the latter, opposed as he was to right and justice. Even so, his understanding eyes had come to her as something of a shock, yesterday; so much more vital and appealing were they than she had recalled. San Saba Lee was going to be a knot in her clear thinking such as he had never been before.

So it was that Rhoda's mood did not appreciably lighten when the man himself rode toward her across the brown plain, his candid gaze on her face as he drew near.

"I reco'nized youh fog horse, ma'am," he told her apologetically. "You don't mind?"

She was looking at him levelly, as though seeing him for the first time. "Where are you going, San Saba?"

"Why, I was comin' to see you folks! I told you." His tone was faintly hurt that she should have forgotten—or had chosen not to remember.

"Oh . . . But Jess is not at the herd; nor Billy," she said gravely. "Only Glen."

He was still watching her speculatively. "I like Glen," he confided gently.

"San Saba, what is going to become of us?" she

demanded abruptly, turning in her saddle. "You can see both sides of this fence, can't you?"

He met her unwavering hazel eyes for a moment, rendered thoughtful. "Lo'd he'p me, it's one fence I can't th'ow my saddle on!" he voiced his reflection. "But I can see the grass on both sides!"

"San Saba, do you believe Colonel Purdy—and the Englishman—are within their rights?"

"Why, I know the Kunnel is, ma'am. He's proved on his range. An' I suspect the Spade outfit of not bein' far behind. But whether they're in theah rights, wo'kin' togetheh, is somethin' else again. One fence, alongside of one fence, in that place, is consid'able mo' than just two fences."

She drew in her breath slightly. "So they are working together now," she murmured disspiritedly.

San Saba changed front quickly. "No, ma'am. They're not," he said positively. "I saw to . . . But they will be, in spite of all anyone can do," he went on. "I'm downright sorry to say that Kunnel Dick wants to. Ma'am, I hate that wire like poison! Even Kunnel Dick dislikes it . . . I've tried to persuade him. But he is iron."

They had swung their ponies, and were riding slowly back toward the Catlin camp, side by side. She was watching him, her eyes luminous. "San Saba, why don't you talk like this to—Jess and the others?"

"It would put me on theah side," he said simply.

Something hard came into her gaze. "You give yourself away there, I think. You would not make Jess a straight answer yesterday. Perhaps you will me. Are you against we small grazers in this dispute?"

"No! No, ma'am!" His denial was vehement. "I ce'tainly am not! Don't you go thinkin' sech a thing!"

Her brows cleared, but the puzzlement in her mind was evident. "But you say that you are not for us; not on our side——"

"Now!" he interrupted her eagerly. "Heah's where the split comes! You've hit it plumb centeh, ma'am! . . . I ce'tainly *am* for you, all the way! Only I can't be on youh side—I've got me a job. Don't you see?"

She gave away to petulance, her perplexity unappeased. "San Saba, why don't you throw up that detestable 'job,' and follow your own sentiments?"

It brought him to a jarring halt. "I can't, ma'am; I simply can't. I wish I could!"

"You say you—can't?" she persisted uncertainly.

"No." His voice was soft, but his negative was definite.

"But why? Why must it be this way?" The frank appeal of her eyes exceeded that of her words. "What are you going to do? You must see . . ."

He saw with a secret leap at his heart that she had espoused his problem as though it were her own.

"I can ce'tainly see plenty!" he confessed with a touch of grimness. "Right now I see myse'f between the devil and the deep sea. But ma'am, with things tightenin' up, it'll he'p to have some kind of a go-between. This thing'll never be settled with guns to anybody's satisfaction."

"No," she admitted reluctantly. "But how can you answer to yourself? I can agree that you should see our side to be in the right! You are not exactly without brains . . . But how your faithlessness to Colonel Purdy can make the free-rangers believe in you any more readily——"

"No! Ma'am, you won't see!" His tone of remonstrance was emphatic. "There's right on both sides, and I couldn't be loyal to anybody and still ignore·it! *You* know what happened last night, don't you?"

"Yes. Henry Chiles rode out. He told us."

"And that's just a lick to what'll come, and keep right on comin'!" he went on quickly. "Don't you see what I'm drivin' at? *Sidin'*, one way or the other, is just what's goin' to carry this on an' on. Fairness and agreement are the only things that will stop it!"

"Fairness——" she began, and paused.

"I know what you are goin' to say. Ma'am, human nature is a critter, and fairness a star. I don't expect to persuade anybody to it, except in a gen'al way. But if you can get them to accept what they think is it, and ev'body is satisfied, it's as much as the Lo'd himse'f has any right to ask."

Rhoda was silent for a long minute, and when she turned to him her eyes were rich with pain. "The most thankless task on earth, San Saba!"

He was staring ahead with lean, graven features. "If I can get it to wo'k, I won't worry about the gratitude. I'll be takin' my pay anotheh way."

"You will," she said on a new note, which made

him harken keenly. "You'll be drawing it in large installments of universal contempt . . . No! San Saba, you've no right to set yourself such a task. It invites disaster—it will mean your finish!"

He refused to consider the matter dramatically. "I don't think it's as fatal as that." He shook his head slightly. "Don't you bother, ma'am." He was contemplating the lazy brown curls at her ear now, his mind scarcely on the subject.

"And so you are coming out of this, famed, respected, trusted—if not dead?" she said sharply.

He looked at her quickly, startled. "Something like that, ma'am," he answered then, his brief smile discounting any charge of arrogance. To distract her mind, he ventured a new subject: "Have you—if you'll excuse me, Rhoda—have you seen Billy since last night?"

She met his look attentively. "No. Billy hasn't come back—since."

He dissembled his close interest in her answer. "I was wondering where he was."

"Jess has gone to look for him," she went on. "He was supposed to have returned with Mr. Chiles. San Saba, do you think Billy is in danger?"

He did not explain that his concern for Billy was seated in that individual's potentiality as a firebrand. "He'll be back. And Rhoda—ma'am—he shouldn't! He should go away somewhe'es for a while. I thought maybe if *you* was to say something to Jess, it would get to Billy in a way that he'd listen to——"

Rhoda cooled perceptibly. "I don't know why you should concern yourself——" she began.

"Girl, I've got to!" he caught her up sternly. "Don't you go to thinkin' I'm doin' it for love of Billy—or for hate of him eitheh!" His flesh reddened, under the healthy tan. "If it's for anything, it's for love of you. I'll say that heah and now! . . . What I *was* getting at," he went on, "is that if I'm goin' to do anything, I can't affo'd to overlook a bet! And I've got to have he'p. Rhoda," he broke off gravely, riding close; "you can see now what I'm tryin' to do. *You've* got brains too! Will you th'ow in with me—he'p me where you can? We'll lick this jackpot, an' walk away smilin'! I know you can do a lot . . . if you will."

Rhoda gazed ahead, her hands together on the saddle horn. A sharp wave of feeling assailed her. Was he making his appeal to her heart, or to her intelligence? She could not be sure. Before she could commit herself to a reply, an interruption occurred which altered the mood of the moment with swift certainty.

San Saba emitted an unconscious grunt which drew her eyes to his face, and then sent them sidewise across the sun-drenched plain to where he was looking. Several miles away she descried, riding over the prairie at a steady trot, three men of unpromising aspect. Their hats were down, firm; the rifle barrels across their saddle-bows glinted. They were converging on the Catlin camp. The "dog house" was visible, a mile away on the bank of Lost Cabin Creek.

"Who are those men?" Rhoda demanded apprehensively.

His answer was reluctant: "It *looks* mighty like Arapahoe Jones, Jackson an' Brazil, from the Spade outfit. Ma'am, if you'll touch up youh horse, we'll get to camp ahead of them."

"They've come for Billy!" she exclaimed, as the ponies mended their pace.

No more was said as they drew near the camp wagon ahead of the three men. Still at work on his quirt, Glen looked up, smiling. He too, had spotted the approaching riders, for his glance went back to them fleetingly as he got to his feet.

"Few of the Spade boys," he observed quietly.

"Seems like," San Saba assented.

San Saba and Rhoda dismounted. In another minute the Spade men drew up, a dark, compact trio, unsmiling. Their curb-chains jingled easily.

Arapahoe Jones' regard traveled over the three, pausing perceptibly on San Saba. Then he spoke briefly, clipping the colorless words off:

"Billy here, Catlin?"

"No," said Glen.

Arapahoe's hard eye lingered on Rhoda. "He ain't out with the steers either, I don't s'pose?"

"No."

"Any idee where I'll find 'im?" Arapahoe persisted bluntly. He was a stocky, pugnacious figure in the saddle.

"Don't you answer that, Glen!" Rhoda exclaimed, her eyes flashing.

Glen merely met Jones' look with thin contempt, unresponsive.

"Aw—plug the coyote!" Denny Jackson growled harshly, his rifle stirring. He began to swear blistering oaths under his breath. "By God, *somebody's* goin' to pay for Gene!"

"Where *is* Billy?" Arapahoe bawled suddenly, his features darkening.

Glen only shook his head, his gaze hard.

"Jess, then—damn you!"

Rhoda interrupted, crying: "They are not here! Go away, all of you!"

Neither Arapahoe Jones nor the others were listening to her. The former and Glen were fighting a duel of stares. Suddenly Jones' arm flashed out, the finger pointing:

"You've got no gun. Git one!"

"Whut the hell does he need a gun fer?" Denny Jackson put in hoarsely. His rifle came up.

But it was Link Brazil's six-gun that barked first. Rhoda screamed, backing into the *palomino*. San Saba grasped her arm with a steadying, iron grip.

Glen's belt and gun lay on the let-down steps of the camp wagon. He whirled toward it with a flashing face, still grimly silent. The resonant detonation of Jackson's rifle echoed, and Glen fell headlong. He was up in an instant, desperate.

San Saba yelled warningly, to no avail. Link Brazil

extended the forty-five and sent four ringing shots at the boy, one after another, remorseless. To the accompaniment of Rhoda's repeated scream. Glen sank down, still a dozen yards from his gun.

It was over in a moment. Then the three Spade ponies were drumming away in quick leaps.

"Dear God!"

Rhoda broke from San Saba's restraining grasp to run sobbing to her brother's side. There she sank, horror in her eyes. San Saba followed her more slowly, but with tense, strained face, perspiration standing out on his forehead.

The girl whirled on him with a gasp of searing repugnance.

"Leave us! Go away!" she almost screamed. "San Saba Lee, I hope never to see you again!"

He recoiled sharply, staring in amazement at her flaming face.

"Rhoda!" The ejaculation was wrung from him. "Couldn't you see—don't you know——?"

The futility of it struck him sharply. Slowly, with gray face and trembling hands, he turned and walked toward his pony, the shuddering quaver of the girl's grief ringing in his ears.

CHAPTER TEN

BUFFALOED

SWINGING into the saddle, San Saba knew that circumstance had caught him up decisively. Rhoda had been right! There could be no more arbitration for him—no more fine reasoning. He had underestimated the forces at play beneath the surface of the range feud. He had led Rhoda into unwarning peril that had dried his mouth and left him cold and immobile, and had won her hysterical contempt as well.

It presented him with a bitter duty that he had no thought of avoiding.

With a rocky face he rode out on the range in search of the first Pitchfork man he could find. He had no difficulty in locating Smoke Chaloner. The middle-aged cowboy rode toward him slowly.

"Chaloner, go back to the camp wagon," San Saba instructed. "Glen has been shot by some of the Spade boys. Miss Rhoda'll need you."

Smoke's face went taut and strained. "An' I didn' even hear the shots?" he burst out amazedly. He began to swear in deep, full tones. "Lee, where're *you* goin'?"

"I don't know," San Saba answered shortly.

Chaloner was far from satisfied: "Wal, did you have anythin' to do with this, Lee?"

"No!"

Turning his face away, San Saba did not wait for further parley with the chagrined puncher. Neither did he ride with him toward the camp wagon on the creek. Striking off at a tangent, he passed the camp widely and rode for a mile into the east. Then he quartered until he found the clear trail of Arapahoe Jones and his companions.

This, he saw before he had gone far, led straight toward Fetterman. Having satisfied his mind to that extent, he gave himself over to gloomy reflections.

"Poor Glen neveh knew what was comin'!" he mused bleakly. "He neveh had a chance . . . Damn Jones, an' all his tribe! I'll hamstring him!" And after a heated interval he resumed: "She'll neveh look at me again. She didn't have a ghost of a notion of what was hangin' oveh her head!"

He knew to a certainty that the course he had taken had been the only one that could have saved her life. Holding the upper hand, the Spade men had been merciless. They had come for unquestioning vengeance, and they had taken it. If San Saba had given them the shadow of an excuse, they would have shot down Rhoda and himself with pantherish readiness.

Had it not been for her presence, San Saba would have met them unhesitatingly with deadly fire. He would have gotten some of them, too, before he and Glen were both wiped out.

"It wouldn't matteh if it had been that way—but she'll neveh see that side of it," he burst out hope-

lessly. "All she could see was her brotheh goin'
down . . . It was hellish!"

It made him toweringly angry with Billy Catlin, who
had precipitated the tragedy. San Saba shuddered inwardly at the thought of his folly in asking her to aid
him. He was no better than Billy, attempting to drag
her into violence in which no woman had any conceivable place. She was in danger this minute; and
would be increasingly so.

"Jess ought to do something about that," he told
himself with miserable conviction. "He's man grown,
and knows his duty. But if he don't, I'll do something
about it myse'f!"

Approaching Fetterman, he looked ahead with grim
determination. It was midday, and the sun flooded the
crude buildings and corrals with unsparing revelation.
The street was plentifully sprinkled with switching,
dispirited saddle horses. A three-team freight outfit
was unloading before the principal mercantile estab-
lishment. A stage was pulling out on the eastern trail
with jingling concord chains and snapping blacksnake
whip.

San Saba's eyes sharpened at the figure he saw sliding crabwise into a nearby saloon. He got down before
the place, and hitching the pony, strode in. He found
Billy Catlin at the farther end of the bar, his back
turned to the door.

"Wha'd'you want, San Saba?" the latter demanded
truculently, as they came face to face.

San Saba had all he could do to snaffle his leaping

anger with the man. "What are you doin' in Fetterman, Billy? D'you know wheah Jess is?"

Billy swaggered. "Shore I know! He's in town now, Lee—an' lookin' fer me! But he don' know *I'm* here, an' you won't tell 'im, either!"

San Saba's features darkened. His hand flashed out; he grasped Billy by the shirt front and drew him forward with a jerk.

"Listen, you young fool! You don't know the hell that's campin' on youh trail this minute! Out at youh herd, Glen is layin' daid, shot by Arapahoe and Jackson and Brazil—all on your account! D'you get that? Glen is *daid,* and youh sistah come near it! An' right now, them Spade men are in town lookin' for you too! If you've got a lick of savvy you'll hie out of this fast, and go a long ways!"

He thrust Billy away. The latter caught himself, his back against the bar, and glared his implacable resentment.

"Damn you fer a liar, Lee——!" he began in a trembling voice.

"You heah me!" San Saba thundered. Surprised men backed away from them, mouse-quiet, wary.

There was nothing the matter with Billy's nerve. Conviction came to him in a rush. Fire crept slowly into his cheeks, and San Saba read the thought that dawned in his brain.

"Don't you draw on me, you hellion!"

But Billy was incorrigible. The other saw that he had gone past reason—that there would be no stopping him, short of decisive action. He unconsciously afforded San Saba time by launching into soul-scathing invective.

Before he had whipped himself to the point of striking, San Saba's six-gun came flashing out. Up—up— his arm raised, and then down, a swift, chopping blow.

His own gun half out, Billy straightened, stiff. A blighted look flitted across his countenance. Then with a sliding crumple, he stretched out on the boards of the floor, unconscious.

"Good Lord! He's plumb buffaloed 'im!" a bartender ejaculated hoarsely.

Another came hurriedly around the end of the bar; but when San Saba whirled on him, he stopped short. The Tincup foreman's hard gaze swept the saloon.

"Have you got a back room handy?" he snapped at the barkeep. The other had. "Ve'y well. Tote this man in and let him lay. He won't botheh you any. He'll come to and fade . . . You heah me?"

Satisfied on this score, San Saba strode toward the door, his manner grim. Brushing through the batwings, he came face to face with Jess Catlin, Hank Chiles and Bitter Creek.

"Lee, have you seen Billy?" Jess demanded.

A cold wave of warning went over San Saba. "Suppose you find out, Catlin!" he retorted sternly. He brushed past, eyeing Bitter Creek, in the rear, with an unwavering regard.

Jess was blasphemously nonplussed. He swung,

frowning, toward the door. "Whut's been doin' in hyar?"

San Saba had not found time to stop and explain. Aroused to a fighting pitch, and nearing his quarry, he was of no mind to be stopped now—to be distracted by anything.

"It's damn queeh!" he thought peevishly. "A minute ago I'm lookin' for Jess Catlin. Then I snap his haid off!" After a moment he continued: "He's bound to find Billy, though. And Billy will tell him . . . If I know as much as I think I know, Arapahoe an' his thugs won't keep!"

San Saba halted abruptly. His eye had caught the Spade brand on a lathered pony standing at a nearby rail. He turned to the saloon before which he stood.

Michael & Mann's was generously patronized today. He heard the murmurous hubbub and guffaws of men at the games and the bars. He stepped up and entered, so intent on what lay before him that he did not see the nine men who crossed the street behind him, following him closely.

He knew the Spade men, drinking recklessly to their violent coup, would be waiting for him, or for anyone who came as he did, with sweeping gaze and careful, straight-hanging hands. Then, he saw them.

They were ranged along the left-hand bar. They turned on him quickly, waiting for what was to come. San Saba stopped, raking their blunt faces with an unshrinking curiosity for sign of the ability to do what they had done.

They were, however, in no hurry to repeat the operation. Moreover, the man who faced them now was not unarmed.

"What've you got on yore mind, Lee?" Arapahoe Jones demanded softly. "Let's hear you say it!"

"He'll say nothin'!—Git over there, with yore damn blacklegs!" a strident voice behind San Saba broke startlingly upon the room. "We'll settle this our own way!"

Simultaneous with this outburst, San Saba received a violent thrust that sent him stumbling toward the Spade men. Flinging a look over his shoulder, he saw the angry faces of Billy Catlin—Jess—Hank Chiles—Bitter Creek—others.

"Hang on, there!"

"Hang onto this, you skunks!"

"Git down, Lee—for God's sake!"

Swiftly the impassioned cries and retorts sounded, punctuated by the thunder of guns in the enclosed place.

For a moment it was pitched battle, with men dodging, flinging shots feverishly, and cursing with frenzied excitement. Except for the combatants, and those pinned in corners, the saloon was cleared with unprecedented celerity.

San Saba did not know exactly what happened, except that lead flew promiscuously and glass crashed. Before he could swing around, he felt a hot slash across his ribs. He fell flat, as though he had been knocked down, his face striking the floor a blow that all but blinded him. More shots racketed, and the acrid odor of burned powder bit his nostrils. A hand grasped his arm and yanked him up roughly. Dimly he saw the granite features of Arapahoe Jones.

"Lay off!" he roared his exasperation, whipping his body around as he jerked free.

"Git out of here!" Arapahoe bawled heatedly. "We're goin'!"

The free-rangers angled away from the brightness of the door, where they were silhouetted. Their figures were no more than half-distinguishable in the thickening gunsmoke, but Billy's curdling cries and Bitter Creek's warwhoop were unmistakable.

Across the bar-room Arapahoe, Denny Jackson and Brazil ran crouching. They did not delay to contest the ground, dodging through the door and out.

"There's one more of 'em!" Hank Chiles' bull-like call rang warningly.

San Saba took one fleeting look and dived. He made the door unscathed, then stopped stubbornly and backed away, his gun in his hand.

Shouts sounded up and down the street, a louder, authoritative bellow among them; but San Saba gave no heed. Hoofs pounded, and slowed; and glancing sharply, he saw Arapahoe, mounted and leading his pony by the rein. San Saba sheathed his gun and grasped pommel and stirrup. The forward surge of his spooky mount swung him into the saddle. Side by side the ponies hammered after the receding figures of Jackson and Brazil.

"Damn you, Jones———!" San Saba could trust himself to no more.

Behind them the free-rangers emerged to the porch of the saloon. One or two final shots banged futilely.

"They'll have somethin' to explain to th' marshal, anyway!" Arapahoe exclaimed tersely, as the two ahead slowed to wait for them. Link Brazil was staunching a furrow across his scalp, and Jackson tenderly examined his thigh.

Still San Saba could say no word, his feelings in turmoil. His tight face was like granite, the darkening bruise on one side of it raw and crusted. How circumstance had manhandled him in a few brief hours! *He* —not Billy Catlin—had been buffaloed.

Bitter as he felt toward Arapahoe Jones and his heartless companions, he could not now carry out his original intention of facing them down; calling them to account; gunning them as they had gunned Glen Catlin. Barbed wire bound them together with bonds of steel, setting them in common defense against the enraged free-rangers.

But he was determined that he would be no party to the inhuman methods of the Spade brand. More than ever he was determined that Colonel Purdy should not join forces with this cut-throat band. When Arapahoe Jones accosted him gruffly, breaking in on his baffled preoccupation, San Saba lashed out at him savagely:

"Curse you, 'Rapahoe—I nevah thought I'd live to see a man do what I've seen you do to-day! You'h a mis'able skunk, an' you can heah me say it! And fu'the'more, the next time you see me, come asmokin' —because, damn youh eyes, that's the way I'm acomin'!"

He snapped his teeth down on these words uncompromisingly, and with a frozen stare, turned his pony out of the trail to ride away alone.

Arapahoe glared after him with furious eyes.

"That's orright fer you, Lee!" he called out wrathfully. "And in the meantime, you better decide which side of this fence yo're on! I've got my eye on you! You c'n bet I don't love you neither! . . . Come asmokin' or any other way, you bench-legged pup! We'll send you home in a wagon!"

It was as though San Saba had not heard, jogging across the prairie in the direction of the Tincup, his lips compressed.

CHAPTER ELEVEN

THE SPADE BIT

THE home ranch of the Great Plains Cattle Co. was as spruce and modern, in the sense of strict utility, as Christopher Mackey had been able to make it in some nineteen months of altering and renovation. Built on a slight rise at a bend in the South Fork of Feather Creek, it was a welter of corrals and buildings.

The Spade ranch, so-called after the monogrammed H D brand, which the Great Plains Co. had taken over, normally presented a busy scene. Chickens ran and scratched in the ranch yard; ducks waddled near the creek, or floated in the eddies. Milch cows wandered in the pasture; blooded saddle stock stamped and snorted in the corrals.

The main building was a long, rambling accumulation of additions, of painted white pine, in one end of which were the resident manager's ascetic living quarters; and in what had been the original H D home, the large office, where all the business of the ranch was transacted. The rest of the building was given over to guest accommodations, feed and store rooms, and in the far wing, the bunk room.

This morning the office screen slammed and Chris Mackey stepped out on the porch just as Beefy Rankin sloshed the dirty water from his dishpan outside the cook shack. The manager was in his shirt sleeves, and bore a quirt in his hand.

"Rankin, where are those men Jones brought out from Fetterman last night?" The cook could easily see that Mackey was in no genial mood, his mouth drawn down.

"Why, they're in the bunk room luxuriatin', boss. You want 'em?"

"I do."

Beefy hastily set down the dishpan and started for the bunk room, wiping his hands on his smudgy apron. After a sharp glance in the direction of the corrals, Mackey turned back into the office.

Five minutes later two burly men shouldered past the screen awkwardly and faced the manager across the desk on which lay his quirt. He did not ask them to sit down, nor did he get up himself.

"You are—h'm—Wagoner and O'Malley?"

Van Wagoner rumbled an assent, and for a moment no one said anything further. Slowly, carefully, the three measured one another. Chris Mackey's normally red features were lean and shrewd. His keen eye strayed, as though by chance, to the double guns on both of the men before him.

"I suppose Arapahoe Jones has told you something of the conditions that prevail here?"

Wagoner nodded heavily. " 'Bout the wire, an' Gene Rule cashin' his chips—if that's what you mean." His breathing was audible in the quiet office.

Mackey was thoughtfully thumbing an unlighted

cigar butt which he had picked up from the desk. "Of course you know I don't want just a couple of cowboys," he said suddenly.

Tex O'Malley stirred slightly, smiling, and Wagoner looked back from the window at Mackey. "You ain't got 'em," he assured tersely. His knuckles rested on the edge of the desk. "Hell, man!" he went on gruffly. "You don't have to pussy-foot with us."

"No?" Mackey's rising brows revealed his desire for time in which to think. "You're both cowmen, I take it."

"An' so're you," Van rejoined immediately. "This is a cowman's game. Don't be worryin'! . . . What d' you want, anyway? Somebody plugged?"

Mackey did not so much as flinch, rolling the cigar butt in his fingers, gazing at it. "Not particularly. I've put up a fence. I mean it to stay there! . . . Of course I don't know what it will cost anyone else," he added harshly. "That's up to them."

Wagoner grunted, glancing stolidly at Tex O'Malley. "So what're we, then. Fence guards?"

Mackey glanced up at last. "You can put it that way if you want. You understand it's your brains, as well as your time, that I'm hiring. What I want is results. And I'm not offering double pay for trying, either."

Wagoner had not removed his ponderous regard from the Spade manager. "Jest what d'you mean by results?" he queried.

"Whole fence! And an end to this business! . . .

You have a pretty accurate idea of what is brewing, I daresay," Mackey broke off crisply; "or if you haven't, you'll learn. I," he went on decisively, "want a stop put to this wire stripping, and the running of cheap, scraggly stock onto our range. I can't afford it! No one else is going to take advantage of this land that we've preempted; and no one is going to drive trail herds through here, regardless. I don't care *how* it's been in the past!

"You can consider those conditions as constituting your instructions, and govern your actions accordingly. I don't care a tinker's damn how you accomplish it!" He sat back in his chair, striking a match, and turned the half-cigar in his lips as he lit it.

"Suits me," Wagoner said at length.

Mackey looked inquiringly at O'Malley.

"Shore," said Tex easily.

"All right . . . And Wagoner——" The Spade manager leaned forward as the two men turned to leave. "Bear down on those swine!" he bit off sharply, his gaze hard.

Wagoner did not trouble himself to reply.

For half-an-hour after his new employees had gone, Chris Mackey sat in his chair, his shrewd gaze calculating. He threw his used cigar out of the window, bit off the tip of another and lit it, still plunged in thought. Then he rose abruptly, purpose in his movements.

Colorado's head popped around the corner of the blacksmith shop at his hail from the porch.

"Saddle the dun gelding for me," Mackey directed.

"Shore." The cowboy came forward. "Boss, our south fence was cut las' night."

Mackey snarled in his throat. "Don't bring it to me! Tell Wagoner, in the bunk room, or wherever he is . . . Was much of it pulled out, Colorado?"

"Naw. Jest somebody passin' through."

The intelligence met with no approval in hard, gray eyes.

"He's got the bit in 'is teeth orright!" Colorado grumbled as he went after the dun horse. "Spade bit at that . . . Haw!"

Ten minutes later the Spade manager splashed through the creek and headed west at a fox trot. Unmindful of the heat, he wore Norfolk jacket and Stetson, sitting the saddle with efficient ease.

Colonel Purdy accosted him from the gallery of the Tincup ranch house an hour later:

"Good afte'noon, Mackey! Get down, seh. So Lee has got to you already! I was expecting to ride oveh to the Spade ranch this evening."

"Lee?" Mackey swung down smartly, trailing the reins. "Haven't seen the man. I came on my own responsibility, Purdy."

The Colonel's eyes sought his face. "No? That's queeh. I sent him——"

"Let's go inside where we can talk," Mackey interrupted coolly.

"Ce'tainly, seh! Ce'tainly," Colonel Dick responded hastily. He led the way into the library.

Glancing up the hall as they passed through, Amantha Purdy sniffed. She did not like Christopher Mackey, and made no pretense of welcoming him.

"Well, Christopher!" The Colonel settled into his second-best chair, the Englishman having selected the other.

"Damned unwell, Purdy!" Mackey began without preamble. "I never saw such a bloody heathen land in my life! Australia's a haven of refuge to this . . . You heard about my rider being killed yesterday? Shot down like a dog!"

"Why, yes! One of my boys brought the news." Colonel Dick hesitated. "Things are gettin' wo'se every day. I suppose something's got to be done about it."

"Done!" Mackey was half-resentful, wholly irascible. "Certainly it has! I've already done more than a little . . . Have you had any trouble so far?"

"Why—nothing but what my fo'man has been able to talk away. I've been right proud of him up to— last evening. What he means———"

The Colonel stopped vaguely, still rasped by San Saba's parting shot of the night before. He had given considerable thought to the matter since then. His foreman's diagnosis of the reason for the erection of the Tincup range fence was in fact the true one. Stiffnecked in his own way, Colonel Dick had prided himself that no one could possibly guess the fact. Yet San Saba had penetrated it with decision. Was it as apparent to this man before him now?

"We built fence for a definite reason," Mackey was

saying dogmatically; "a good enough reason for it to remain there! I'll be damned if I am to be browbeaten in this God-forsaken country! If it's dog eat dog, I am as good a mastiff as the next!"

"Well—that's true, pe'haps. These are strange people, Christopher. A little tact——" Mackey snorted, and the Colonel hurried on: "Not but what you've got to hold up youh haid, you unde'stand. You can't expect much from the territorial gov'ment until it gains weight. But I thought if things get much wo'se —the military at Fo't Fetterman——" He had begun to talk fast under Mackey's intolerant stare, but now stopped, rather angry with himself.

"The military! I tell you, Purdy, this can be no case of hit or miss! We're not a—lost wagon train!" Mackey barked scornfully. "I know *exactly* what we have to contend with! This is a legal desert, infested with rapacious savages! There is no semblance of law —no conceivable hope of order. What law we recognize we have got to make for ourselves!"

"But, my dear man——!" And when Mackey waited, stern, Colonel Purdy pushed on: "We aren't living heah absolutely alone!"

"That's precisely what we are doing! I think you confuse the issue, Purdy. If you will stick to cases, and consider these hairy renegades as nothing more nor less than the obstacles they are——"

"Why!" Colonel Dick was openly astounded. "That's horrible!"

"—you'll deal with them accordingly!" Mackey

completed smoothly and grimly. "And you'll produce results! That is the sole purpose for which I'm living in this wilderness!"

"Why—that's as much as saying that if I accidentally got in youh way——"

Chris Mackey shrugged deprecatively, tossing out a hand.

Colonel Purdy was increasingly perturbed in the presence of this hard, uncanny man. He remembered San Saba's reluctance in agreeing to join forces with Mackey. It struck him to wonder whether Mackey had not indeed divined the secret behind the erection of the Tincup fence, and if he were not using the knowledge to his own advantage. Colonel Dick sat straighter in his chair.

"I believe I unde'stand now. What is it that you propose, seh?"

"Consolidation! Throwing our forces together!" Mackey barked. "Meeting these blackguards along a common front. I've already begun to take on new men——"

"But that means complete agreement in ev'thing," Colonel Purdy pointed out slowly. "It means one aim, and one responsibility for all that happens . . ."

"Of course! Why not?" Mackey's brows lifted. "The wire gives us common cause—thrusts it upon us, to say the least! Come now, Purdy! Don't shilly-shally with me! Speak your mind, man! I'm willing to have it out with you!"

"And have youh own way, afteh!" the Colonel coun-

tered explosively. At last he began to perceive what
the man was about. His face darkened with blood.
"No, Christopher; I'm far from satisfied——"

It was at this moment that a light step sounded at
the door, and a spur tinkled. San Saba cleared his
throat softly.

"Excuse me, Kunnel. I'll look in on you lateh," he
said apologetically.

Colonel Dick scrutinized him sharply. "So you're
back, seh! Was there anything heah you come afteh?"
His coolness was marked.

"Why——" San Saba was thinking fast. "Not unless
it's Mist' Mackey, Kunnel Dick. I hadn't got to him
yet. But you said tonight——"

"Oh." The Colonel frowned but relented. "Come
in heah, San Saba. Wheah've you been?"

"I was at Catlin's camp, on the Lost Cabin—with
Arapahoe and a couple of his men." San Saba stopped
with just the right shade of embarrassment. "They
went oveh to speak to Billy."

Mackey sat forward in his chair, his face keen.

"And did they—find him?"

"No." San Saba shook his head gravely. "So they
shot young Glen to make up for it," he launched the
easy words into an astounded silence.

Colonel Purdy rose as though on springs. "They
went oveh there and *shot* Glen, San Saba? The three
of them?" The lines in his face deepened. "Why, *he*
didn't have anything to do with that business yeste'-
day! . . . Did he do any shootin'?"

"He didn't have a gun on him," said San Saba simply.

"Fiddle-sticks!" Mackey broke in upon the strained pause. "I daresay the fellow got exactly what he deserved!"

The Colonel whirled on him in anger. "You don't know what you'h saying, Mackey! I know youh men are consid'ably roused. But this hot-headed, cold-blooded shooting is no light matteh . . . As to ouh joining fo'ces, the word Lee was to give you was that I'd see you about it tonight. I'll confess myself still unce'tain about it in my mind—but now I'll ask you to give me until tomorro'. Until then——" He paused expressively.

Mackey jumped up, his face a deeper red. He gave San Saba a bad-tempered stare, his quirt twitching.

"Very well, Purdy! But don't make any mistake! You think it over damned seriously, and be sure you decide the right way!" He stood upon no ceremony, striding toward the door. "I'll be expecting you," he said curtly, and was gone.

San Saba looked after him. Colonel Purdy contented himself with an impatient grunt; but when his foreman's eyes returned to him, he was still scowling his displeasure.

"San Saba, was you *with* those Spade men at the Catlin camp?" he got out distastefully.

"Why—no, suh," San Saba answered awkwardly. "I wasn't."

"Well . . . that's something," Colonel Dick commented dryly. But the gaze with which he continued to regard San Saba was far from free of suspicion. "What was it you was doin' oveh theah, if I may ask?"

And when San Saba did not reply, Colonel Dick went on sternly, "I haven't yet made up my mind what to think of that rema'k you made last night."

Still San Saba stood silent, turning his hat round and round, his manner studious.

"Ve'y well, you stubbo'n, long-eared Texas mule!" Colonel Purdy burst out furiously; "tell me what you came to say, or else get out of heah!"

Strolling toward the bunk house, crooning a melancholy saddle song, San Saba grinned to himself and felt immensely better. Colonel Dick had as much as admitted himself to be in the wrong. He would be irritable and distant for several days; but San Saba believed that he had won his point.

CHAPTER TWELVE

DECLARATION OF WAR

THE little band that rode away from Fetterman behind Jess and Billy Catlin was a grim one. Although they had resisted the heated accusation of the marshal, after the brush with the Spade men in Michael & Mann's saloon, he had sent them packing with a belligerent warning.

Jess, however, could not ignore an older grievance. He persisted in airing it with dogged ire:

"I *told* you to meet me at the river, an' bring Hank, hyar, along with you! But no—you forgot what I said the minute you was out of sight! . . . Anythin' fer a little more hell, dang yore brass!"

"Who'd'a guessed I was goin' to run into Packer trailin' a herd south?" Billy retorted imperiously. "I wouldn't've missed that fer you, or fer anybody!"

"Wal, you could've tried to argue Pack out of it, then, couldn't you? But did you try?"

"He was goin' with Hank after 'is stock! I told you that!" Billy cried.

"Did it help any?" Jess demanded with biting emphasis. "You saw us git turned back—an' then you helped Pack to git throwed out! That's how much good yore blasted shootin' did! You say *no-o*, Rule can't be dead; but I bet you he is, or them fellers'd never drilled Glen like that—dang you an' what yo're goin' to do all by yoreself!"

Riding up beside them, Hank Chiles put in forcefully: "That's right, by Godfrey! They ketch us a few at a time, an' they make fools of us! Jess, yo're dead right!"

Jess glanced at him in grudging approval. "Shore!" he rejoined impatiently. "How long'll it take you fellers to see it? If Billy'd said somethin' to you—or if you'd used yore head—you'd had the sense to hang fire until we was *all* ready to move! Now we been kicked around aplenty, an' we've got *them* all stirred up! Like as not, they'll be waitin' fer us, an' jest honin' fer trouble, next time we show up!"

"Wal, that's fair enough!" Billy whipped out savagely.

"Yo're damn right it is!" Hank Chiles concurred with equal gusto.

Behind them Bitter Creek was animatedly haranguing the sympathetic cowboys who had taken part in the Fetterman fracas. All quieted, however, when the "dog house" at Catlin's camp hove in view over the last swell. More than a few hats came off as they dismounted and moved forward.

Rhoda sat dazedly on the steps of the camp wagon, her cheeks colorless. There was something stricken and unearthly in her tearless gaze which made the men shame-faced. As they neared in a hushed body, she rose and stumbled into the shadowed interior of the wagon.

Glen was lying on a blanket where Smoke Chaloner had placed him at Rhoda's direction. A portion of the blanket was laid over his face, telling the newcomers all they needed to know. Jess folded the covering back and they gazed at the dead man with solemn faces.

"Plugged half-a-dozen times!" Hank Chiles muttered gruffly. "They shore didn't leave nothin' to chance."

Billy's face was flushed and angry, his jaw thrust out. He was telling himself that he proposed to leave nothing to chance either.

Little time was lost in ceremony. Glen's eyes had been closed. Jess crossed his hands and proceeded to wrap him in the blanket. The others turned away to gather in a group at one side, murmuring in subdued tones.

Smoke Chaloner came walking toward them, a spade in his grasp. He had dug a grave on the crown of the ridge. His weathered features were sullen, and he had little to say. He had liked Glen the best of the three brothers.

They buried the latter almost immediately, with simple dignity. Half-a-dozen men carried the body up the slope. Rhoda stood by, her suppressed but shuddering sobs rendering the silence poignant, while they lowered Glen into the grave.

"Thar's little that I can say," Jess intoned in a muffled voice, his eyes hurt, his nostrils pinched. "He was a good boy. Brother an' companion, he done his work an' kept 'is head. It's a—it's a plumb dirty shame to have to plant him now. He wasn't ready to go. But if God's in the saddle, He's lookin' down hyar—an' He'll know whut to do. An' that's enough."

The shovel clinked on dirt, and Rhoda turned quickly away. They watched her with pitying eyes. Scarcely a man but felt her grief keenly.

"It's a dang crime!" Bitter Creek burst out, as Smoke methodically completed the heaping of the mound. "Chaloner, d'you know what happened here?"

"Wal, she—Rhoda done told me in jerks, without me askin' her," the latter said heavily. "Seems the Spade men come rarin' up lookin' fer Bill. When they couldn't find him, they throwed down on Glen. Then they helled off."

Billy flung up to them tempestuously. "Smoke, did you see it? Did Lee come out here with them?" he blazed.

"Why, no! I didn' see it—or Catlin, likely I wouldn't be here now—but the girl said he come with her. They met some'eres on the range, an' got here 'bout the time it happened."

"Why didn't Lee do somethin'?" Billy persisted hotly.

"Hyar, now!" Jess broke in shortly. "He was with Rho', you fool . . . Smoke, didn't Glen put up a row?"

"Wal—she said he dived fer 'is gun. But he didn' git to it."

"*What!*"

"The stinkin' skunks!"

The look on almost every face was one of wrathful

contempt for the Spade men. Even Billy was taken aback.

"Didn't the fool have 'is gun *on?*"

"Hold on, now, Hank! Glen's dead," Jess reminded hardily. He was beginning to see many things that before had confounded him.

Chiles was profanely amazed. "By God—that settles it!" he exploded. "If them hounds think a little wire's goin' to hold us back——!"

"Shore!" Jess thrust in grimly. "We all feel that same way. But don't you go mixin' things up, Hank! I'm jest beginnin' to see daylight. . . . San Saba was high-tailin' after them birds when we seen 'im—an' we pushed him plumb into 'em!"

"Yah—he was!" Billy interjected scornfully. "That's why he lit into *me* like a wet wolf!"

"Wal—Lee went off with the Spade fellers, in Fetterman!" another pointed out.

"Why don'chu ast the girl what San Saba was doin'?" Bitter Creek put in shrewdly.

"I will," Jess decided suddenly.

"An' while yo're about it, you listen close!" Billy rasped thinly. "I don't put no stock in none of them lobos—an' if you know what yo're doin', you won't neither! They'll pull any of us down if they git the chance! You think Lee was coverin' Rho'—but I'm tellin' you he was coverin' himself! With her here he knew better'n to make a move, because he knew we'd find it out! You better turn that over fer a change!"

"You hush up!" Jess rumbled commandingly. "Yo're

allus startin' somethin'!" But the expression in his eyes as he strode toward the camp was far from satisfied.

He found Rhoda behind the camp wagon, her back against its chipped and splintered panel. Distracted, inconsolable, she did not know what to do with herself, gazing off across the creek with wet, unseeing eyes.

"Rhoda—girl—this is plumb tough! But we've got to face it, an' no flinchin'. . . . Will you tell me whut San Saba Lee was doin', hyar, when them fellers rode up?"

Her cheeks flooded suddenly with scarlet. "He was standing behind me—beside me—I don't know! Jess, he did nothing!" Her voice was tragic. "It was . . . terrible!"

"Didn't he make a *move?*" Jess demanded harshly, his eyes searching her face. ". . . Didn't any of you know what was comin'?"

"I don't think so—we knew suddenly, when it was too late," she amended troubledly. "San Saba yelled—something—he grabbed my arm. I believe I would have rushed at them! But he didn't move. . . . And then they were gone." She avoided the actual scene with painful care. "I hate him!" she burst out then. "I never want to lay eyes on him again! Oh——!"

She turned away abruptly, and stood with head down, her shoulders shaking. Jess walked around the wagon biting his lips, and met the others with heavy eyes.

"I can't say *whut* I think!" he blurted, his voice

husky. "She—she thinks Lee backed down on it, pulled leather."

"Wal, the question is, what *we're* goin' to do, Catlin!" Hank Chiles thrust in gruffly.

The men gathered around, their faces keen.

"Shore—give us the lay, Jess!" Bitter Creek seconded. "I guess we're all willin' fer you to rastle the hackamore—till you begin to haul in!" He glanced about. There was no dissent.

Jess nodded. "I won't say much now. It's bob-wire we're tanglin' with. That means ever'body's got a say —an' we ain't all hyar. We don't want any more damn pirootin'!" He considered deliberately.

"I move we have a pow-wow some'eres, where we c'n all git on our hind legs an' have our howl. Not hyar." He jerked his head backward toward the wagon significantly. "But some'eres where we'll all git thar. . . . Whar's yore herd, Hank?"

"Over on the river," Chiles answered. "Pack's an' my bunches're jest one scrambled mess. Pack's thar now, crusty as an ole bear, figurin' what to do."

"He got his boys with 'im?"

"Shore. Len Bain, an' Cheyenne."

"An' Old Blue?"

"We sent him to the doctor, over at the Fort. Arm all swelled up, an' sore's a bile. But he'll be along."

"Wal." Jess was coolly abstracted. "We c'n meet thar at the herd, then. Say tomorrer night. That'll give us time to round ever'body up. That orright with you boys?"

Assent sounded on every hand.

"Shore," said Chiles readily. "An' Jess, you be shore an' bring Brush, an' Smoke an' yore Injun. We'll need all we c'n git."

"We c'n lay over at the herd, an' push it ahead of us when we git our plans made an' start off in the mornin'," Bitter Creek volunteered with satisfaction.

"What—an' give 'em another chance to kill off a lot of steers?" Billy countered impatiently.

"Don't you go losin' yore head, Bill!" Bitter Creek told him sharply. "I know what yo're fixin' fer. . . . If we barge down there by our lonesome, lookin' fer war, we're li'ble to meet up with a flock of sojers! Cattle's our excuse fer needin' that range when we come to it. We don't want to overlook a bet!"

"I don't give a *damn* about a few more dead steers!" Hank Chiles thrust in concurrently. "That wire's what's got me sweatin' the leather! We're due to clean the range of the stuff—an' that's whatever!"

"An' in the meantime, you badgers stick to business!" Jess cut across their bickering with hard intent. "If you'll jest circulate back to Fetterman an' gather the boys, we'll know whar we stand. Don't figure this to be no lark! What we want is a squar deal, an' no shenanigans!"

All agreed to this with harsh bluntness. A few minutes later those who did not belong at the camp were on their way back to town in a compact cavalcade. Once they had got beyond earshot of Catlin's wagon, the sobriety of the occurrences there was forgotten. An air of grim jubilation prevailed, on the part of the younger men—of reckless anticipation in the face of the promised campaign against the abomination of the barb-wire.

CHAPTER THIRTEEN

DOGSOLDIER IS CURIOUS

RUBBING the back of his burly, leather-colored neck experimentally, Dogsoldier Olsen cocked a blue and cheerful eye at the street of Fetterman. He had just faced successfully the ordeal of a horse-clipper haircut, and was at peace with the wide world again.

"Hey, Dogsojer!"

Olsen turned as speedily as his enormous bulk would permit, and found at hand his old friend, Len Bain.

"Dogsojer, I was lookin' fer you. I'm plumb afoot fer cash. Let's go have a drink," the latter engagingly proposed.

"Dot's yust vot Ay ban tankin' myself!" Dogsoldier responded. "Ay go you, Len. Let's go in here an' have von."

They turned into the nearest saloon and had von. In a few minutes, at the suggestion of Len, they adjourned to a second saloon and had another. This was continued in a somewhat erratic rotation, until Dogsoldier was removing his broad-brimmed hat at intervals, and patting his well-nigh denuded poll to remind himself of his altered condition.

There was no mention of barb-wire. Dogsoldier told with zest how the tonsorial operation had been accomplished; how the clippers had struck this bone and that, and glanced off. He told how the stableman had grasped his ear, and he had bit his tongue and hung on. He was (now that it was over) the soul of amiability.

So was Len Bain, until he had imbibed what Dogsoldier considered to be enough for any man. They were in the street, scarcely a brace of doors from Michael & Mann's. Dogsoldier did not appear to see the slim figure of Billy Catlin pausing in the door for a moment, and glancing back at them—but he did. Also he saw the highsign which Billy tipped to Len before he disappeared.

He was immediately curious, but he gave no indication of it.

Len started for Michael & Mann's on the double-quick; then bethinking himself, he hesitated, turning back.

"Huh?" said Dogsoldier vaguely.

"Durn you, Dogso——" Len stared at him suspiciously. "Whut're you followin' me fer, anyway?"

Dogsoldier looked confused. "Ay don't—hic—follerin' nobody, Len!" His tone was injured.

"Wal! Jest see you don't!" Len bristled pugnaciously. He swung away and strode with dignity toward the saloon, muttering to himself.

Dogsoldier stared after him, blinking.

"Ay ban sure curious about dis!" he muttered dully. "Len, he ain't so drunk as dot, naw. Dot Catlin faller ban up to somet'ing, Ay tank, yah!"

He was still standing there when he perceived another acquaintance advancing from the other direction. It was Bitter Creek.

"Hallo, Bitter Creek!" Dogsoldier greeted him effusively. "Ay ban yust tank about you. Come on have a drink wit' me! Ay feel lonely."

Bitter Creek put on an expression of surprised gratification. "Why—uh—shore, Dogsojer! Right in here, ol' top!"

They had their drink. Bitter Creek picked up the second, set it down again, and then suddenly turned on his companion. "Jings! Dogsojer," he explained confidentially, "I done got a job. Jest remembered it. You jest wait right here, an' I'll be back. Savvy?"

"Yah! Oll righ', Bitter Creek. Ay——"

But the latter had not waited for an answer. He was gone, leaving Dogsoldier to stare at his glass in struck silence. Then, recovering himself, he glanced up in time to see, through a side window, Bitter Creek stepping with excessive casualness into Michael & Mann's.

The huge Swede was lonely no longer. He was highly entertained, if somewhat mystified. What was going on in the other saloon?

It piqued him. Dogsoldier was a conscientious man. It was that quality which had earned him his nickname, and he was not long in putting two and two together. When half-an-hour had flown by on leaden wings and Bitter Creek did not return, Dogsoldier had decided upon his proper course. It was a simple one. Weaving out of the saloon, he started absently for

Michael & Mann's. There seemed to be some question as to whether he would get there.

At last he reached the porch. It was waist high, and he navigated it with care, hanging on for dear life. It was a study to watch him pull himself up to a sitting position thereon. He seemed to fall asleep, his back supported by one of the pillars of the wooden awning, his head on his bony knees. Flies buzzed about his nose and crawled in the stubble behind his large, red ears, but he masterfully did not notice them.

He was debating the advisability of wandering into the saloon, when the group of free-rangers emerged.

"Don't fergit to tell Bandy, now," Billy Catlin was saying importantly to Len Bain; "an' anybody else you run acrost. T'morrer night, at Pack's——"

"Shet up!" Bitter Creek growled. He indicated with his thumb Dogsoldier Olsen, whom he had spotted immediately. "You don't have to tell all you know!"

"Blast you, Bitter Creek!" Billy was inclined to be quarrelsome.

They were interrupted now by a fresh development. Upon their ears, as upon those of Dogsoldier, there broke a striking, a memorable, voice:

"Wal—look who's hyere!" Unctuous gratification sounded in the harsh words.

Dogsoldier Olsen opened one eye. Standing before him, with hands on hips and legs spread wide, was Van Wagoner.

"Tincup waddy, ain't you? I shore been lookin' fer you a long time, big fella!" Wagoner growled, taking a step forward, and knocking away the support from under Dogsoldier's head with no gentle thrust. "Better late than never, I guess!"

"Huh?"

Olsen jerked awake, bleary-eyed, and all but fell off the edge of the porch. Billy Catlin guffawed hugely, and Len Bain grinned. Bitter Creek, however, grumbled shortly:

"Aw, leave 'im be. Can'chu see he's oiled?"

Wagoner remained unimpressed. "Whut's it t' you, waddie?" he snapped at Bitter Creek. His jaw thrust out belligerently.

"Aw, hell!" Bitter Creek rejoined disgustedly. But he offered no further participation in another man's business.

Van swung back to Olsen, purposeful and vicious. "Stand up an' look at me, you blasted hunk!" He laid hands on Dogsoldier, attempting to drag him off the porch.

"Wait, now! Ay—Ay yust——" the latter articulated with difficulty.

"Yah—you yust!" Wagoner yanked at him wickedly. "Come down hyere, squarehead!" He would not have offered to touch Dogsoldier at another time. Now he appeared half-scornful. "Big man! San Saba Lee's right bower, eh?"

Dogsoldier came down off the porch asprawl, his weight sagging in Van's clutch. His knees buckled, and he breathed a richly perfumed breath into the other's face. Wagoner slapped at him vigorously as he slumped.

"Come awake, you slob!"

"Hey!" Bitter Creek ejaculated contemptuously, his lip curling.

"Damn you—I *told* you!" Wagoner blared wrathfully. His hands were unexpectedly full, but he stared over Dogsoldier's head meaningfully. "Speak up—or dust! I happen to be workin' fer the Spade outfit right now, if you wanto make anything of it!" His tone was one of the utmost provocation. If Van noted the slight stiffening of Dogsoldier Olsen's body, he gave no sign of it.

"Ay tank maybe—my legs——"

Bitter Creek again subsided, with morose rumblings of protest, and watched with fascination what was taking place before his eyes.

Dogsoldier's freckled, beam-like arms were around Wagoner's trunk, and as he progressed steadily downward toward the dust, each of them snagged on his supporter's guns. Van suddenly thrust the Swede violently from him, with a furious grunt; and as they parted, both the man's six-guns tumbled out and bounded.

Wagoner bawled, his face flaming. Dogsoldier was ahead of him, however, having the advantage of being nearly on a level with the fallen firearms.

"Ay get dem—for you," he got out thickly. He grasped one in each ham-like hand, despite Van's madly stamping boots. Then, wobbling and flushed, he lurched up.

Wagoner rushed at him like a crazed steer, oblivious of the chortles and jeers of the delighted free-rangers and others. Dogsoldier's knees threatened to desert again, and for a moment the two men staggered wildly, clutching each other. Wagoner was rapidly losing all semblance of composure, shouting frenziedly.

"Hey—ah-h!" Bitter Creek shrieked his glee. "Bull-dog 'im, Dogsojer!"

Dogsoldier did. It was a kind of exaggerated bear dance, without design or apparent result, but highly diverting.

Suddenly one of the guns went off. The bullet ploughed into the dust at no great distance from Wagoner's right foot; but a large portion of the audience did not pause to note this interesting fact. A second after the explosion, most of them were engaged in traveling rapidly hence, though few passed beyond convenient earshot, and none beyond the relatively clear view offered by doors and windows and the angles of adjacent buildings.

Van Wagoner did not desert his post. He did not dare to. He howled and snatched, jumping backward and forward and sidewise; to little avail. It was significant that for all their intricacies of step, his hand did not come within reach of Olsen's own dull-handled forty-five, reposing innocently in its holster.

Dogsoldier's knees, oddly enough, no longer displayed any alarming weakness. It was his arms that waved and sawed, like high limbs on a storm-tossed oak. From time to time a fresh explosion sounded, and lead ploughed the ground or the atmosphere. Dogsoldier was chanting a lugubrious melody of the ranges, the staves of which he punctuated with enthusiasm and abandon, a silly expression on his face.

It was the distant appearance of the marshal of Fetterman, rather than a dearth of six-gun ammunition, that put an end to the exhibition. One look and Dogsoldier's arms came down; his body swayed; his face returned to wonted bland opacity. Van Wagoner regained the six-guns at the first savage snatch.

"What's goin' on yere, anyways?" the irate marshal demanded authoritatively. He was a lank, capable, if bilious soul. "This gazabo ridin' you, feller?" he flung at Van.

Wagoner's visage was murderous. "No!" he spat out poisonously. He earnestly desired to make no more of a show of himself at present.

"Wal—somebody's to blame yere!" Marshal Brogan insisted peevishly. "How many times've I got to tell you boys that I won't stand for no ranickaibos?"

"Oh—go hang a crepe!" Wagoner snarled in a muffled, trembling tone that was just barely indistinguishable. His face was the color of an old saddle. He jerked away in a towering rage.

Dogsoldier was more amenable to persuasion. "Hon —honest, Marshal, Ay vas yust—yust havin' little fun," he protested weakly. "Ay ban going home now. Ay—Ay von't do it no more, yah!"

"Wal, see to it that you don't!" the incensed up-holder of the law snorted. "If you think I'm gonna be satisfied with *talkin'* to you blasted three-year-olds——!"

"Ay—Ay tank Ay be good, maybe, yah!" Dogsoldier conciliated lamely. He was weaving in the direction of his tethered pony. Putting a hand to his head for the benefit of all chance observers, he groaned and muttered thoughtfully: "Oh-h, Ay ban sure got a head! Ay must 've drunk somet'ing, yah!"

"Yeah—Ay tank!" a derisive voice responded.

Dogsoldier took off his hat and patted his crown again, tenderly and solicitously. But the thing that was on his mind, as he rode swaying out of Fetterman a moment later on the long trail to the Tincup, under the appreciative eyes of Bitter Creek, Len Bain and others, was something much more disturbing than the coiling fumes of low-grade whisky.

CHAPTER FOURTEEN

COLONEL DICK SAYS NO

DOGSOLDIER made an excellent blacksmith's assistant. He could hold down a pony's head with one hand, and a hoof between his knees was steady as rock. San Saba was as grateful for this as for the news the huge Swede gave him while they labored together in the little smithy on the Tincup in the cheerful light of the morning.

"It ban plain enough, San Saba," Dogsoldier rumbled over the sizzling of a hot shoe. "Ay tank dey have a meetin'. Pack ban pretty hot boy when Ay ask him for a match, at the Platte. Ay yust make sure. He ban waiting for somet'ing, all right!"

Mirthful glints shone in San Saba's eyes after a hilarious recountal of the drunken scene in Fetterman the previous afternoon. "Yes, it ce'tainly sounds like it," he agreed. "You did fine, Dogsoldieh. I'll sho' be theah. Now," he continued thoughtfully, "if I only had somethin' real arrestin' to say to those boys——"

Dogsoldier was struggling with another thought. "San Saba," he began hesitantly, "that Van Wagoner ban a bag egg, yah!"

San Saba's level eye was on him. "I reckon he is, Dogsoldieh. Bad enough."

"Yah, a bad egg," Dogsoldier reiterated, scratching

his head. "What has he got against you, San Saba?" he went on suddenly, his eyes shrewd.

"Me?"

"Yah—you." Dogsoldier was not abashed. "Ay get an idea it's you Van's got it in for. 'San Saba Lee's right bower,' he ban call me, an' whack me again. . . . Do you know Van, San Saba?"

The latter's eyes were quizzical. "Yes, I know him."

Dogsoldier grunted. "What did you do to him, to make him so mad at you, San Saba?"

The Tincup foreman mused for a moment before replying. Then, in a temperate voice, he told the big Swede about the Texas trail boss who had stolen his employer's money. "That's why I'm heah now, Dog-soldieh—to make my uncle's money good—and to meet that trail boss again. Van Wagoner is him!"

Dogsoldier's eyes bugged out. "San Saba, you ban goin' to meet that man—face him down?"

"I am." San Saba was sententious. "He'll not get away from me a second time, Dogsoldieh!"

At this moment Pink Robinette stuck his head in the door. "Boss is yodelin' fer you, San Saba," he announced. "I think he's r'arin' to lay you out."

"Fine!" San Saba threw down the hammer. "In that case, you c'n just he'p Dogsoldieh finish his hoss, Pink."

He grinned over his shoulder at Pink's crestfallen expression.

Colonel Purdy was strolling the ranch house gallery,

serious of mien. He stopped, rubbing his hands as San
Saba approached.

"I've got a job for you, my boy," he said decisively.
"You can ride oveh to the Spade ranch and tell Christopher Mackey that I say no to his proposal."

San Saba suddenly grinned. "No?" he echoed.

"No," the Colonel confirmed. He snorted. "I suppose
you think it's funny or something?"

"Lo'd love you, suh; it'll be easy for me. Not to
mention the pleasuah!"

Colonel Dick flushed. "Whenevah Mackey loses, you
think you win!" he barked. "Just be suah you are not
flip with him, you scamp! He's got to know *I* mean it—
not you!"

San Saba sobered. "I'll save him any worryin' on
that score, Kunnel Dick," he promised. "Of cou'se you
don't mind my calmin' him down afteh he heahs?" he
went on innocently. "He's bound to blow some."

Colonel Purdy appeared about to erupt. "Get out of
heah, you unpredictable blackleg!" he shouted, fuming.

San Saba waited to hear no more, heading for the
corral. Five minutes later he rode away from the ranch
toward the gate in the range fence which opened upon
the Spade ranch.

"Kunnel Dick says no!" he breathed to himself.
"Nothin' between us an' the Spade outfit, except distance! I guess that's somethin' like ammunition to use
at this free-range meetin'!"

He was light-hearted, riding through the clean, blue
and gold morning. It had stormed during the night, and

the strong sunshine, flooding the sagebrush, drew into the air the tonic resinous tang of new growth. The green-tinged Laramie hills bulked above the prairie with pleasant sharpness of outline. Along the horizon, fleecy cloud galleons tugged at anchor.

San Saba's pony was mettlesome, head up and hocks flying. Everything, it seemed, was to his taste. Only when he remembered the death of Glen Catlin did a shadow flit across the features of the Tincup foreman. Life and death rubbed shoulders, in this lusty land, with an astonishing democracy.

He let himself through the gate upon Spade land and rode on. As he gazed toward Feather Creek, he thought of Arapahoe Jones, whom he had forgotten. Was Arapahoe waiting for him at the Spade ranch? He realized that he had dug a pit for himself, in warning the Spade foreman of their next meeting. But perhaps Arapahoe would be somewhere on the range, and they would not meet.

It was not Arapahoe Jones from whom San Saba had the most to fear this morning, however. He was unaware that from the time he got a mile inside the Spade line, he was under the surveillance of a far more dangerous man.

Riding up over a swell, Van Wagoner had spied him instantly. He yanked his horse in and watched keenly, an expression of ferocity leaping into his heavy face.

"Lee!" he grated harshly, under his breath. Though he had learned of San Saba's position, it was the first time he had seen the other since the affair at Fetterman weeks ago. But the old hatred was as potent as ever.

A red curtain filmed his gaze, and he tightened his grasp on the rifle he held.

"Gad! Half-a-mile down the hump, here. . . . I could knock him off jest as easy!"

Wagoner turned his pony and pressed forward in haste, keeping the swell between San Saba and himself. When he reached the point at which he judged the other would pass within a hundred yards of the crest, he slipped down and crept forward, the Winchester at his side. Near the top he lay down, crawling through grass-tufts and sage, his gaze darting ahead.

He had guessed accurately. In another moment, San Saba rode serenely forward within easy range. Wagoners' rifle came up. Then he hesitated, staring at his intended victim through the brush. Nervously he debated with himself, while San Saba drew steadily nearer.

"How'll it look?" Van argued, fighting the mad desire to shoot first and think later. "Purdy's foreman has got no argument with Mackey! I expect they're friends! . . . God! It'll look bad!"

He trembled with the lust to kill, holding himself with uncertain hand. The rifle rose again, wavered. Sweat broke out on his face.

"Mackey'll pin it on me in a minute!" he gasped. "That Swede'll tell! . . . Dammit!" he raged inwardly. "Why don't I blaze away, an' rattle my hocks outa this country? I c'd make it!"

But something told him that he had already waited too long. San Saba had passed him by. If he shot him now it must be in the back. Then if anything went wrong; if Wagoner should be apprehended before he won clear, it would look worse than ever. . . .

He followed San Saba for several miles, in a ferment of fear and desire and self-disgust. Again the rifle peered out of the grass toward the Tincup foreman; but not again did Van get the priceless opportunity he had had at first. And always the vague repugnance at back-shooting made him hold his fire.

He watched San Saba approach Feather Creek and splash across; and when the other passed from view amidst the ranch buildings a magnetic impulse drew him forward still. He followed warily, approaching the ranch by a round-about course, savage of mood but knowing his hands were tied.

San Saba found Chris Mackey in his office.

"If you'll pahdon me for supposin' I know somethin' about youh business, Mist' Mackey, I'll say that Kunnel Purdy sent me oveh with a message for you," he said.

Mackey sat forward expectantly, missing the veiled gibe. "That so? I trust Purdy'll be over sometime later to confer with me on arrangements." He was almost affable.

"Kunnel Dick says no," San Saba went on quietly. "We all know what that means. The Kunnel has decided that it would be bettah if we big outfits fight ouh own battles by ouhselves."

Mackey's stern visage became suddenly saturnine.

"You needn't explain anything to me, Lee!" He rose abruptly, bumping his chair back. His eyes flashed. "So Purdy has decided to buck me!" he jerked out.

"Well. . . ." San Saba demurred.

"Never mind!" Mackey cut him off. "Your opinion is of no account whatever!" He gathered his forces for a blasting dictum. "By Heaven, he'll not get away with it!" he ejaculated harshly. "Putting me off, and then throwing me down! Who does he think he is? . . . You can tell him that I'll be over to see him about this! He'll change his mind, all right!" He held himself well, unconvinced as yet of defeat.

San Saba countered tersely: "You needn't botheh comin'. Because you'll neveh get to Kunnel Dick, Mackey, unless he wants it. . . . I can speak fo' him. Now get this right: We are not youh enemies. And neitheh are we youh shock-troops! You might as well get oveh the notion!"

Mackey exploded then, as San Saba turned toward the door. The latter had no joy in this man's company and, his ultimatum delivered, wanted to leave it. The Spade manager bawled after him from the open screen:

"You think you're bally high-handed, Lee, but I'll teach you different! Don't forget that I've got something behind me besides a bunch of cowboys!" San Saba's imperturbable acceptance of this gave him a fresh impetus, and he flamed wrathfully: "And just for something to think about, you insolent hound, you can tell Purdy that I'll see him tangled in trouble if I have to go out of my way to do it—if it's the last thing I do!"

The angry words echoed through the ranch yard. San Saba harkened, frowning. "I'll tell him," he replied, so quietly that his tone itself was a contemptuous rejoinder. He went on toward his pony, considering the import of Mackey's impassioned outburst. "Did I say somethin' about ammunition fo' this free-range meetin' tonight?" he mused grimly.

At the corner of the ranch building he almost bumped into Arapahoe Jones, coming from the other way. Both stopped, frozen to the ground. Arapahoe's clawed hand hung ready, waiting. For a moment no word fell. Each measured the other inscrutably. San Saba was wondering with annoyance how he could avoid bloodshed on the spot.

"So you changed yore mind, eh?" Jones growled finally.

San Saba's face darkened. "I have done consid'able thinkin', 'Rapahoe," he responded. "But don't let that hold you back," he invited coolly.

Arapahoe's lip curled. He knew how to take advantage of the scruples of men. "So you think you'll get down off yore hoss an' crawl a while?" he went on harshly.

San Saba did not lose his temper. "You know whether I'm crawlin' or not, Jones!" he said softly. "I was sho' plenty hot yeste'day. But I've cooled off." They matched stares for a moment, and San Saba went on: "I told you I'd done some thinkin'. It don't mean

I've changed my mind about you! I neveh thought I'd
live to walk around a man that's done what you
did——"

"What'd I do?" Arapahoe demanded bluntly.

"You know, 'Rapahoe! Brazil an' Denny Jackson
ran a blazer on Glen Catlin an' left him layin'; but
you took them oveh there. You was in charge. An'
you'll pay for it! . . . That's why I've changed my
mind. I'll just make sho' you know, an' let you sweat
awhile! Man, you couldn't get away if you wanted to!
Why should *I* bring the Catlins down on my haid by
takin' away from them what's ce'tainly theahs?"

"Yah!" Arapahoe blustered, bolstering his disbelief.
"That's purty good, Lee! That's figurin' yoreself out
of it, all right, all right!"

"So . . . ?" San Saba rejoined, in a tone that made
him jump. "If you want to figuah me back into it, it's
youh deal!"

Jones scoffed, grasping his safety with eager hands.
"Why should I meet you, now or any time?" he
snarled, brazenly turning away. "If I'm the kind of a
buzzard *you* think I am, I c'n knock you off when I get
ready. You better do some thinkin' about that, Lee!"

Listening at the other corner of the ranch building,
Van Wagoner could have kicked himself for his weak-
kneed hesitations of an hour before. If he had only
known! Lee's ill-favor here at the Spade ranch; his
sharp difference with Jones, would have been cast-iron
alibis for Van, were any needed!

Beside himself with rage and disappointment, Wagoner watched while San Saba strode to his pony under the baleful scrutiny of Arapahoe Jones, and swinging up, rode out of the ranch yard as calmly as though nothing had happened. There was no sign of the intense satisfaction the Tincup foreman had gotten out of his morning's work.

When he passed from immediate view, Wagoner ran feverishly to his pony and flung himself into a stalking pursuit, his eyes smouldering like those of a cougar, his nerves cold and set. But to his exasperation he got no more chance at San Saba, from behind or otherwise, this day.

CHAPTER FIFTEEN

BETWEEN TWO FIRES

YELLOW twilight cloaked the range when Jess
Catlin and his little outfit splashed across the
Platte toward the camp of Packer and Chiles, ten miles
above the Fort, on the appointed evening. A fire had
been built of driftwood, and a large gathering of men
was grouped around it. All were armed.

These men drew apart in knots, murmuring among
themselves, as Catlin's party dismounted and turned
their ponies into the rope corral near at hand. Stares
were turned on Rhoda Catlin as the girl stood waiting
for Jess. In the lurid mixture of twilight and driftwood
flames her expression was unreadable, but her face
looked pale.

Snorts and muffled exclamations of protest sounded
from every quarter.

"Catlin," Hank Chiles accosted Jess gruffly, "why in
hell'd you bring the gal? Thought you was goin' to
leave her out of it." His impatience was patent.

Jess flung out his hands. "She changed my mind,
Hank," he answered shortly. He advanced to the fire,
a deliberate, assured figure, Rhoda at his side. "Boys,"
he raised his voice, "don't go to losin' yore stirrups!
This business is open to all. It was her brother, was
shot down yestid'y. The girl's a cowman. She won't go

fer leather, an' that settles it. . . . Are we all hyar now? Let's git down to cases."

All were standing around the fire, ready and waiting. Spurs tinkled and cigarettes glowed in the growing dusk.

"Where's the Injun, Catlin?" someone asked.

Jess heard it. "You all know Red's a Shoshone," he responded.

A wave of grim amusement followed the exchange.

Rhoda avoided the watchful eyes, which the men simply could not help. She was provoked with the subtle difference her presence made in the tone of the assemblage.

It was an influence, in fact, rather salutary than otherwise. Younger men withheld their expressions of unbridled gusto, their cries of incitement. All buckled down to earnest sobriety. There was no inclination to treat lightly the object of the meeting. No smiles were visible; no small chaffing of gathered acquaintances was heard. Grim business was the acknowledged order. No one assumed leadership, but Packer and Jess exerted hard, dry guidance.

"I take it thar's no question of whut we're plannin' to do," Joe Brush put forward boldly. "Hit's fight that fence, an' not waste no time about it!"

"Wal—*is* that what you-all figure on?" Jess interposed, with particularity.

"Come off!" "*You* know whether 'tis!" "This ain't no legal case, Catlin!" the exclamations arose.

"Wal, it's this way," Bitter Creek put in practically.

"Purdy an' Mackey're two men. We're twenty-odd—
and ever'-one of us full-sized behind a gun!"

"But don't git the idee it *is* two to twenty!" Billy
Catlin warned harshly, stepping forward. "They c'n
match us man fer man. They got punchers ridin' the
line right now. An' whut's more, the Spade's hirin' gun-
men!" He told briefly of the incident at Fetterman
between Van Wagoner and Bitter Creek, and the big
man's revealing taunt.

Bandy Packer questioned Bitter Creek keenly about
the affair. The latter added what he could.

"I ain't got nothin' against Olsen," he ended, while
men listened closely; "he's a harmless fool cow-poke,
but he totes a gun. . . . I figured if I let it go on,
there'd be a split between the Spade an' the Tincup.
That's jest our meat! Wagoner didn' git nowhere with
the squarehead; Olsen's seven foot if he's an inch;
but Van won't be so easy behind a rifle!"

An ominous rumble, as of promising storm, greeted
the suggestion. In the midst of it, the jingle of curb-
chains sounded, striking them to astonished silence.
They were all here, and expected no one. Who dared
to molest them in the midst of conference?

A stifled gasp from Rhoda Catlin was the first hint
of the identity of the newcomer.

"Lee!—Great Godfrey, what're you doin' hyar?"
Jess Catlin ejaculated imperiously.

The free-rangers stirred, a note of ugliness threading
their response to this audacious visitation. Not a man
of them but believed it to be a piece of bull-bating.

San Saba swung down to meet the several men who moved toward him. He was summarily grasped and hustled forward, to be brought up with a jerk not far from the fire, facing the irate circle.

"San Saba!" Rhoda choked weakly.

San Saba did not look at Rhoda. He was gazing around the ring of faces, sullen in the flickering fire-light. His quick scrutiny ticked off Packer, Jess, Chiles, Brush, and others. Upward of a dozen punchers, however, were unknown to him.

"Lee, you ain't welcome here by a damn sight!" Bandy Packer asserted sternly. "What're you after?"

"Don't let 'im talk!" Billy Catlin flared hotly.

"He's sypin'!" "Snoopin' aroun', 'e is!" "You don't have to guess!" the harsh chorus charged.

"I came heah, Pack," San Saba drawled clearly, "to have my say. An' first I'll say theah's no split between the Tincup an' the Spade, because theah was nothin' between 'em to split!"

Jess cut off the scornful growl that answered this. He faced San Saba squarely:

"Lee, you knowed whar you was comin', or you wouldn't be hyar! Man—you *can't* win! . . . Why'd you step down off that hoss without a gun?"

With blanched countenance, Rhoda stared sharply, cold dread knocking at her breast. It was true. San Saba's lean hips were innocent of cartridge belt or six-gun.

"Because meetin' you boys with a gun, Catlin, is the

same as puttin' on war paint!" he was replying evenly. "I didn't aim to come heah an' fight you!"

"You know whut Glen Catlin got fer goin' unheeled!" Joe Brush accused truculently.

"He *will* know!" Billy flung in furiously.

"Aw——" began a scoffing voice from one side. "We'll see he gits a gun!"

"You *will* not!" Len Bain fired back, bristling.

"Whoa, thar! . . . Lee, is yore gun on yore saddle?" Jess insisted.

"No," said San Saba flatly. He did not mean that it was not there; but—that he would not use it. He still stood with arms transfixed behind him, his wrists clenched. His regular features were pale, his head high.

"Yah—all his sand's in 'is boots!" Cheyenne vociferated. "Flog 'im outa hyere!"

San Saba was yanked around in the backwash of this sentiment. It seemed to Rhoda that fate hovered over his head with frightful uncertainty. She stepped out, her cheeks bloodless, but with the forthright manner of a man.

"Boys," she addressed them coolly, "I came here to hold up my end. I know most of you resent me—and I don't give a continental. That fence is the reason we are all here—not revenge, and shooting, and worse! It was Spade men who shot Glen, when it comes to that. This man has done no shooting; he has done nothing, except talk." Her voice took on an edge of bitterness. "He wants to talk now. If it concerns that fence, let him say what he has to say. Listen to him—

and send him away. Then you can decide what you want to!"

They heard her out with attentiveness. Rhoda stepped back, afraid lest anyone misinterpret her object. San Saba flashed her a look.

"Wal——" Hank Chiles began reluctantly.

San Saba needed no further encouragement. By common consent his captors released his arms. He took a stride out and extended a hand.

"Boys, this is not war-talk. It's an attempt to avoid fightin'. An' the only way to do that is to please ev'body," he said earnestly.

"How c'n you do that?" the scoffing interjection arose.

"This range fence," San Saba went on strongly. "Theah's two of 'em—both an injury to you. I know you've clashed with Mackey. He won't stir a stump—an' I don't blame you-all. . . . Can I ask you not to jump at things? None of youh men've been shot by Tincup boys. Nobody's asked Kunnel Purdy what he's willin' to do. Ouh cows've been shot an' ouh wire stripped. But am I doin' anything but tryin' to straighten it out with you boys?"

Listening scowlingly, Jess Catlin was probably the most impressed of anyone present. He had a sneaking belief in the honor of this man which he could not define. He knew better than to give way to it a second time, however. Billy, Cheyenne, Old Blue and others were growling. The latter spat tobacco juice into the fire contemptuously.

"Git to the p'int, Lee!"

"I will. I told you theah's *two* fences. Don't ove'look that; an' don't mix us up. . . . It's just accident that togetheh, they close off the trail to Medicine Bow."

"What're you gittin' at, feller?" demanded Hank Chiles.

"Tryin' to side us ag'in the Spade bunch, I guess!" snorted Joe Brush. "Thar ain't no split thar—oh, no!"

San Saba's face was flushed. "No! Don't take me wrong! Youh a'gument ain't against the Tincup. It's with Chris Mackey, I tell you! He's a pilgrim; he don't under——"

Ungoverned ejaculations drowned the rest of this.

Bandy Packer's face grew the color of mahogany. "Of all the damned an' ball-headed gall——!" he roared wrathfully.

Others showed their boiling contempt in various ways.

"Wait! Have you *thought* about this?" San Saba's face was like a flame. "Do you *know* whether Kunnel Dick is willin' to open his fence?"

It was a new idea—and a daring one with the Tincup foreman, for he was not himself certain of the answer. But it brought a momentary silence which he was quick to grasp.

"You don't!" he told them bluntly. "All you know is that you want that fence down! I told you theah'd been no split between the big ranches—I didn't tell you theah was an almighty difference between them.

. . . Do you know anything about human cussedness?"

His manner was so gripping that they could not easily discredit it. Keenly they groped to find his meaning.

"You don't any of you act like you did! But you know, all right! Eve'y last one of you has got plenty of it! It's why you'h so willin' to jump at the notion that I'm a skunk because I point my fingah at a man!"

"Nemmind the preachin', San Saba!" Packer retorted darkly. But San Saba was encouraged; it was the first time his nickname had been used, except by Rhoda.

"Boys, think it oveh!" he urged. "One man can make an awful big mistake in this heah country! An' when two men get togetheh on the same mistake——"

"Are you tryin' to say, Lee, that Mackey an' Dick Purdy are on the outs—an' both stubborn about this wire?" Hank Chiles demanded.

"It sticks in theah throats," San Saba responded.

"Haw! . . . Give us'n end of it!" Cheyenne emitted gruffly. "We'll yank it loose fer 'em!" There was no humor in the offer.

"Wal . . . An' so——?" Jess Catlin pressed on shortly.

"Heah's the answer to youh confab," San Saba went on definitely. *"I'm* no fool; an' Catlin, I think pretty well of you-all too. I didn't come heah to bluff you! But you've not had a smidgin' of a notion wheah the pinch comes. It's a blame sight easier to make war out of this than peace. But if you want a man's agreement to youh demands, an' peace at the same time——"

He never finished the sober statement. From out of the darkness rang unwarning shots. No one saw the flashes; no one, oddly enough, was struck, although Rhoda Catlin saw, with a stabbing twinge at her heart, the hat fly from San Saba's head as though snatched; but all were thrown into instant turmoil.

Lurid cursing arose as men pulled one another out of the circle of light with violent hands. Cries of wrath shattered the absorption of the moment before.

Billy Catlin alone galvanized into swift, tigerish offensive action, springing at San Saba Lee.

But San Saba was no longer where he had been standing. When Dogsoldier Olsen told him of the cattlemen's meeting whose hour and scene had inadvertently been dropped, he had wondered whether Van Wagoner had heard. It now appeared to be a fatal certainty. In a split second San Saba sprang away from the driftwood fire toward his waiting pony. Simultaneous with the further spiteful crack of firearms from the encircling gloom, the enraged free-rangers heard his horse's hoofs roll away over the plain in a furious diminuendo.

CHAPTER SIXTEEN

MILLSTONES OF THE GODS

R HODA CATLIN stepped forward to the driftwood fire and picked up San Saba Lee's fallen
hat, which lay in the ashes at the edge of the fire. She
slapped the brim clean with instinctive tidiness, but
gave way to feelings of another order when she noted
the double puncture in the crown. The trouble that
filled her eyes then was a ghost of the dread which had
gnawed at her while San Saba himself had stood here.

She was absolutely alone at the fire now. The silence
was profound, accentuated by the champing of Hank
Chiles' extra horses in the rope corral with her own
pony. She had no thought of her surroundings, however, as she gazed into the encroaching and inscrutable
darkness. The loneliness which assailed her went far
deeper, and was of the heart itself.

She was thinking of San Saba Lee as she waited for
the wrathful free-rangers to return. With the death of
Glen, revulsion at the evident cowardice of San Saba
had torn from her what she believed to be every rem-
nant of her faith in him. Although she could not understand what had made him act as he had. The conviction grew that her judgment of him had been mistaken.
It was a conviction that had leaped to grudging life
at this fire.

"No man who could do what he did here, can be craven!" she declared to herself. "He was laboring for us—against our wishes! . . . I was wrong—wrong— and I have sent him away!"

She knew that San Saba's earnest desire for peace was practically hopeless, hard and dangerously as he had striven for it. Her brothers, and Chiles and Packer and the others, believed him to have intended their betrayal. It did not shake her belief in the man. She felt that she knew what they did not—that it was San Saba's life, and not their own, that had been imperiled by the shots which had come out of the night. It showed in this hat which she had picked up a moment before.

The attack had been as foul and dastardly as that upon Glen; and for this reason she had no difficulty in fixing the blame where she was certain it belonged. The truth of the situation fitted together like the pieces of a puzzle. Although San Saba had tried to shield the Spade punchers, she was not deceived. It had been they who two days ago had killed the thing she loved; and it had been they who tonight had attempted—she now realized suddenly—to do it again.

She had no opportunity for further searching examination of her heart. The men were returning at last, empty-handed and disgruntled. She heard their muttering voices and the soft squeal of saddle leather as several of them drew near.

It was Jess, Bandy Packer, Hank Chiles, Bitter Creek and another, a strange puncher. They freed their ponies and came forward in the flickering glow as Rhoda threw fresh fuel on the fire.

Hank Chiles was the first to see the hat which she had forgotten in her hand. He took a stride toward her and grasped the brim, staring at it. Rhoda retained her hold, watching his face; and when he let go abruptly, her hand fell to her side still holding the Stetson.

Chiles swung back to Jess, his expression severe. "I tell you the gal goes!" he declared forcefully. "There's no doubt about it! Here she is, hangin' on to the feller's lid. . . . Blast you, Catlin, you knowed better!" His tone was surcharged. "Here she got us to listen to th' snake, an'——"

"He's not a snake!" Rhoda flared quickly.

"Wal——!" Hank retorted huffily, at a loss.

"It jest goes to show," Bitter Creek inserted temperately. "She's—'scuse me, ma'am—stuck on Lee. I heard that. . . . She ain't respons'ble," he added with a shrewd glance.

"I am not! I mean——" Rhoda was indignantly near to anger. "He is not what you think! They were shooting at *him*—those men—and they were Spade men, as he warned you!"

"How d'you make that out?" Bandy Packer interposed stolidly.

She thrust the hat out. "This proves it! You can see where the bullet went." Spots of color burned in her set face.

"Aw——" Packer began.

"That was jest a chance, ma'am," said Chiles de-

cidedly. "They couldn't tell us apart at that distance!"
He shook his head disparagingly.

"Rho'," said Jess heavily and with reluctance, "yo're
makin' a big mistake. That boy——"

He got no further. "I think you are all being wilful
and—despicably suspicious!" she flamed swiftly. She
turned and walked away from the fire blindly.

"All the same, that clinches it, with me!" Chiles
insisted, with resolution. "Jess, you'll have to send the
gal away! If it hadn't been fer her, we would've
nailed Lee while we had 'im! . . . Not but what we'll
nail 'im anyway!" he went on.

Jess nodded ponderously. "I see my mistake," he
admitted unemotionally. "She'll go. . . . Soon as these
hyar wild-eyed hyenas git back, we'll make our plans
to git on with this in the mornin'. Likely 'twas the
Spade bunch, orright; but it don't make whose fence
we rare ag'inst. An' it won't be no place for a girl ary
way you look at it," he ended with a curious slow
waggling of the jaw peculiar to him in the moments
when he was aroused.

Wandering agitatedly at some distance from the fire,
Rhoda heard the low-pitched voices of the men. She
paid no further attention to what they said. She knew
the mood that dominated them. It was one of uncompromising and brutal retaliation.

After a long time more riders returned, turning out
their ponies angrily and stamping to the fire with
harsh objurgations. The talk became argumentative
and bitter; but still Rhoda did not return to join them.

Far into the late hours their dudgeon held. Others came in from a longer chase. Still some were missing. Rhoda's impulse was to saddle the *palomino* and ride back to Lost Cabin Creek immediately, defeated and resigned. Jess would not let her. Billy, Cheyenne and one or two other hot-heads who had not returned were liable, he stated gruffly, to mistake her for another. He did not mention the consequences of such an encounter; but Rhoda wearily capitulated.

Carrying her saddle blanket to some distance, she composed herself for rest, using her saddle as a pillow. She had no thought of sleep, staring into the illimitable star-shot void overhead, her soul in torment. The next she knew, however, she awoke to the faint chill of morning air, and dawn light tinged the rim of the east. Someone was kicking together the embers of the dying fire. Rhoda heard the murmur of heavy voices, and knew that the men were already stirring.

She did not wait for the coffee Packer was preparing. Seeking out her brother Jess, she told him that she was going, and at once went to the corral for her pony. There was nothing to do but wait in silence while a puncher caught up Pal for her. She noted now that Billy and the others had returned sometime during the night.

Five minutes later she rode away from the grim camp without a farewell. Pal was thirsty, and she gave him a drink before splashing across the Platte. On the other side she let him graze at a lush grass-patch.

Remembrance of San Saba Lee returned with a stab

as she sat waiting. His hat was caught by the strings at her pommel.

The free-rangers were even now moving at the head of a compact herd toward remorseless conflict with him and his people. What possible outcome could there be except death and sorrow?

She could not conceive, in the emotional turmoil which had returned with full force, why the barb-wire had ever been strung. "I am afraid they were surely mistaken!" she exclaimed agitatedly. But it was not the range fence for which she was apprehensive, but San Saba Lee.

She took heart then. Simplification of that order made for clearer sight. San Saba was, as he must ever be, her essential concern. He had lost her faith, and he had regained it.

"I am *not* a pusillanimous little fool!" she cried, her cheeks reddening. "There was something behind his acts I could not see! He asked my help, and I . . ."

She pulled up the *palomino's* head and sat in fermenting indecision, her gaze turned backward toward the Platte. Despite herself she was daunted.

"I *can't* go back there!" she groaned, her hands twisting together. "One woman couldn't break up all that hate and destruction! Not a one of those Spade men but would prove San Saba right and shoot me down without a twinge!"

All this really weighed for nothing with her. What gave her pause was quite another question. *Should* she follow the insane course which had leaped full-fledged in her brain? Absolutely all that mattered was the certain attainment of her object.

Without further hesitation she pulled her pony around and started back for the river, so impelling was her desire. She drew in when she realized what she was doing, but only for a moment. Then she leaned forward, gave Pal his head and urged him forward feverishly.

The Platte was quickly reached. It was the long, gruelling ride beyond that wore upon her taut nerves. Her pony winded speedily, having drunk too much, and she dared not push it lest it give out altogether.

"Faster, faster!" she breathed an inward prayer. "Faster, faster!" her throbbing pulse beat the refrain. Her distraught gaze searched the range ahead as the *palomino* fought its growing fatigue gallantly and with good heart.

"Oh, I'll never be in time!" Rhoda gasped hopelessly. All her apprehensions were now shaken off. She could think of nothing save the bitter duty she saw, and the danger of arriving at the range fence too late.

At last she came within distant sight of the mingled herds of Packer and Hank Chiles. She strained her eyes, her breath held. Pal struggled onward with ever-slowing hoofs.

The cattle appeared to have escaped control, spread out over a wide area, and they were near the fence. Rhoda's heart sank as she caught glimpses of faint puffs of whiteness through the dust. Above the drum-

ming of the *palomino* she heard the echoes of occasional flat reports.

"They're fighting already!" she ejaculated, her worst
fears leaping in an instant. She set a course toward
the near flank of the herd so that she could still see
what went on beyond.

The great herd had approached the range fence at
a point near the junction of the Spade and Tincup
segments. Howling and determined, the free rangers
had thrown the steers against the barrier almost at a
run—a battering-ram which tore into the strands irre-
sistibly, snapping them and coiling them in gleaming
arcs above the heads of the cattle. Beyond, on the land
claimed by the Great Plains Co., waited a force of
nearly a dozen men, mounted and armed with Win-
chesters.

Hostilities commenced at once. The Spade men set
up a raking fire, concentrating on horses and cattle;
and several free rangers were set afoot within a few
minutes. The others wheeled, their horses rearing, and
fired a vicious response. Dead and dying cattle lay
about, behind which the enraged attackers sought
cover; while the untended herd, aroused by the firing,
and bawling fearfully, backed and milled and kicked,
and began to spread.

On Colonel Purdy's range the free-rangers were met
by half-a-dozen less ruthless, but equally determined
defenders, so that the conflict in a moment became
three-cornered.

Rifles and six-guns were in evidence everywhere.

Shots banged back and forth, infuriated yells arose, and glares of unmitigated ferocity were exchanged, though few except those who had been unhorsed attempted to seek shelter.

"Get busy, thar, an' knock 'em off!" Jess Catlin roared in an authoritative voice. "Then we'll take a turn at this hyar fence!"

The cowboys of the big spreads objected vigorously to such a programme. While it was noticeable that the screaming lead of the Tincup men flew high, that of the Spade punchers did not.

It was amidst this scene of battle, with dust rising to high heaven and frantic warriors busy, fighting gun-shy cayuses and the enemy as well, and the air of an ironic destiny hovering over all, that cursing and consternated men watched the dauntless girl ride boldly down the narrow no-man's-land between the two factions, her head high and her face a pale flame of determination.

"Good God!" Jess Catlin bawled, with unreadable face. "She'll be killed!"

San Saba, behind his own fence, stared at Rhoda, speechless.

The slackening fire had in it no promise of a striking of arms. A wrathy and guttural hail arose from the Spade contingent:

"Whut're you tryin' to run in onto us, anyhow, you blasted yaller-bellies?"

Billy Catlin, Bitter Creek and others exploded in violent retort, and the confusion became general.

CHAPTER SEVENTEEN

ARMED COVENANT

FOR a moment everyone was too stunned by the unexpected to do more than gasp. But only for a moment. Then San Saba Lee set spurs to his dun pony with a grunt. He forced his way past the smashed fence, regardless of the protesting exclamations of Dogsoldier Olsen and others.

Under a battery of hard eyes he rode toward Rhoda, from whose face every vestige of expression had been washed. They met in the open, squarely between the lines of infuriated combatants, and his eye took in the beaten aspect of the *palomino,* lathered and blowing.

"Git outa there!" a harsh command bellowed from the Spade fence. It was Arapahoe Jones, wrathful and vindictive. He followed the explosion with a string of maledictions which made the free-rangers clutch their rifles, muttering.

Neither Rhoda nor San Saba turned their heads. To the nonplussed watchers their attention appeared to be concentrated on each other to the exclusion of all else.

"You might have lost your life doin' this fool thing, Rhoda!" he protested in a lowered voice. A slow flush of indignation burned in his cheeks, high up.

"You risked your own life, last night. . . . Will it

stop them?" Her voice was husky with agitation, and
the reins trembled in her hand, but only he saw the
searching look of beseechment she put on him.

He stared at her wonderingly. "All I ever heard of
you neveh pointed to this!" he responded strongly.

"*Rho'!*" Jess Catlin roared, his face like weather-
furrowed granite. It was neither call nor protest, but
an almighty denunciation.

Billy was not so deliberate. He hated this man who
had ridden in where he had not. Sensing accurately
the awkward shattering of the morale of conflict, he
raked his pony forward at a bound, emitting a howl.

"There goes '*nother* damn fool!" Bitter Creek
gritted angrily. "Whut in the livin'——?" He broke
off to watch.

Billy rode close to San Saba, pulling in with a goug-
ing whirl. Rhoda screamed sharply, once. Then all saw
Billy's forty-five in the air, its barrel slashing down
in a savage blow.

San Saba jerked around, and received the blow
across neck and shoulder. It jarred him. His dun
reared, pawing, while he clung to the rein. He pulled
the pony down, and wheeled to face Billy.

The latter would have attacked again. Jess, however,
had grimly followed him, and now thrust in between
him and San Saba with a rumbling growl.

"Quit it, you young hound!"

The figure that moved out from the Spade group
held both insulation and curbed contempt in its se-

verity. Chris Mackey had presence and force. He addressed Jess without emotion:

"Now that you've arranged your little show, what are you going to do? You think that you fellows can make your attacks, and withdraw, and be none the worse off! I think different!" He gazed with a bright hardness.

Men began to drift forward in varying degrees of sullen disgust and tight-lipped anticipation. Better than three dozen figures moved in, or sat saddle, opposed, at the nucleus of contention. Few relinquished a ready grip on firearms. Those afoot stood together in a resentful group. One or two blood-dampened thighs or calves were noticeable; a Spade man had a kerchief-wrapped hand. Cognizant of the position of their foreman, the Tincup men moved through the press in a silent, watchful body.

Without waiting for Jess Catlin's reply to his thrust, the Spade manager went on hardily: "What the idea of this little scene is, I don't know. Whether it is deliberate or an accident—" he accompanied this with a glance of distaste at Rhoda; "means little. I make no bones of what I am here for—and it is not the chivalrous protection of women——"

"Don't you git overbearin', feller!" Hank Chiles flung in belligerently, from the dismounted bunch.

Mackey regarded him coolly, conscious of the presence behind him of picked gunfighters.

Through the encircling horsemen passed Colonel Dick Purdy. He drew up ten paces from Mackey, and appeared unmoved by the fact that Jess Catlin and Packer flanked him closely. He was the oldest man in the gathering, also the most assured. His refined features were cast this morning in lines of range rock, his manner superb. He cast over all a spell of subtle expectancy. Even Mackey met him with something like annoyed respect.

"Boys," he said firmly, "we're meetin' on thin ice. Theah's no need of lyin' to each otheh—in fact, I reckon any kind of a bluff is goin' to be cold comfort in this gatherin'. What I want to say is——"

"Hold on there, gran'pop!" Arapahoe Jones burst in gruffly. "We don' take no sermon!"

"No! What you want is lead!" Billy Catlin met him truculently.

"You ain't got any to spare, Catlin!" Denny Jackson flamed, holding in his restless mount.

"Wait, now!" Colonel Purdy held up a well-kept hand. "You'h all hot, boys——!"

"An' goin' to be hotter!" Smoke Chaloner growled from the standing group. "Damned if I'm here to listen to ary palaver!"

A mutter of anger arose from the massed riders behind Mackey. Van Wagoner was there, and O'Malley —Jackson—Link Brazil.

"You're not going to get what you came here for— if you care to know!" Chris Mackey bit off.

"How d'you know? What'd Glen Catlin get?" Bitter Creek defied accusatively.

"Wal!" Bandy Packer inserted, "what's the use of

hagglin'? We won't get what we want by askin'. An' we're goin' to have it!"

"Shore!" Len Bain concurred violently. "Let's get into this! To hell with what's left!"

"Boys——!" Colonel Dick attempted once more. None better than he knew that cataclysm hung ready to engulf them. Rhoda was miserably resigned to it, her gaze on San Saba's face.

In the tense silence that followed, the soft crush of saddle leather was distinctly audible. The flat bang of a six-gun had in it something of the suddenness of a thunderclap. Link Brazil, in the Spade group, howled and lurched back against his cantle, raising a hand whose fingers were smashed and reddening. Bleak of face, San Saba pushed forward into the opening in the center. His neck was angrily red from the glancing blow Billy Catlin had struck him minutes before.

"Anybody else's hand itchin'? . . . That was me," he told them all distinctly, his hard gaze roving the Spade men. "I wasn't startin' anything; I was stoppin' it!" His forty-five still hovered in his firm grasp.

"See here, Lee——!" began Arapahoe furiously.

"Wait a minute! . . . Now look heah." San Saba's voice crackled and snapped. His face was cold and tight. "Brazil was flashin' a sneakin' gun on Billy Catlin. I stopped it. Not because I've any love——"

"Why didn' you kill 'em?" Billy flared, his own hand at his belt. Brazil was the man who had emptied a six-gun into Glen.

San Saba gave him a reprimanding glance. "The

question ain't lives—it's fence," he went on clearly. "Theah's nothing in the guns for us now. If we commence, I'll stake anything that half of us go down; but not the fence. . . . You boys," he told the free-rangers, "hang on like death to a niggah—but even you know that we ain't that kind." He paused, reading the faces.

"I've been told," he went on sharply, "that all I do is talk—an' I'm talkin' again. But this time I ain't askin' you to listen! If theah's any one of the passel of you that's got the guts to do it better, let him go to it!"

A disturbance arose among the Spade contingent which Chris Mackey abruptly quelled. Hard as he was, he wanted this thing to end in talk. It would stall the wheels, create a fresh impassé, and preserve the fence. Even the trouble-makers must get used to it in time. Let the Tincup foreman pull their chestnuts out of the fire of he could!

"Now, I've got medicine," the latter began afresh. "Anyone knows this case calls for it. We won't any of us like it, for it's a bitter dose; but we've got to take ouh dose, an' theah's an end of it."

"Name it, first!" one of the free-rangers burst out impatiently.

"Sho' I'll name it. The first dose is to ride away from heah today an' cool off."

"*What-at?*"

"Wal, you ornery——!"

Mutterings, laughter in which there was no mirth,

sounded below the outcry. When they stilled somewhat, San Saba went on: "I've got a plan, an' when
I——"

"Name it!" the protesting voice insisted violently.

"—get a chance, I'm goin' to lay it befo' you-all.
The way you are now, not a one of you'd listen to
anything on earth. I know it. You know it! Nev'theless,
it's a good one—an' what's more, it gives us all what
we want. Does that strike you fightin' bobcats any?"

A babble of derogation and argument arose amongst
the free-rangers. It was easy to see that San Saba had
struck sparks from them.

"Wal!" Denny Jackson's opinion sounded among the
Spade murmurs; "what we want is somethin' doin'!"

"Shore!" Arapahoe took him up. "Let Lee spill 'is
scheme! We'll decide on it blame quick! Ten to one it
ain't nothin' worth listenin' to anyway!"

"If it ain't, I'll satisfy you afteh, Jones," San Saba
promised thinly. "We all know what *you* want."

"What do I want?" Arapahoe blazed back.

"Boys—Mackey—Catlin—San Saba's right!" Colonel Purdy put in loudly, above their hubbub and bickering. "Theah ain't a one of us but is het up, an' we're
provin' it! No reason to chuck good sense. Now what
d'you-all say?"

"What d'*you* say, bob-wire? That's what!" Joe
Brush rejoined gruffly.

"Why, I say let's hit on an agreement!" the Colonel
came back quickly. "We'll call this off, an' then we'll
get togetheh in a quiet way. Caspeh schoolhouse, to-

morro' evening. No guns allowed in the building, an' a regulah meeting. That's faih, ain't it?"

"More talk!" a Spade man snarled heatedly.

"Where're you headin' in this, Purdy?" Bandy Packer demanded.

"Well, you'll learn, seh. Not that I know what's in San Saba's haid this minute. But I know that boy, an— I judge—so do you-all."

"Yeah! We know 'im!" Hank Chiles was referring to the incident of the night before.

Although the response was one of general discontent, it was not a flat refusal. Encouraged beyond his expectations, Colonel Dick pressed his persuasive arguments. He tried cajolery. He appealed to everything in these men that he knew how to reach. Cautiously at first, then with better heart, Jess Catlin coincided with the Colonel's views and brought his sober influence to bear with his men. Chris Mackey waited grimly, cynically; assented now and again dryly, and—waited.

In the end it was grudgingly agreed that the meeting should be held at Casper schoolhouse, ten miles away across the Platte, on the evening of the following day. There the question of the range fence was to be thrashed out and a compact struck which would be acceptable to all.

"Though how we're goin' to hit on one is beyond me," Colonel Dick admitted to San Saba as they rode back through their fence and headed for the Tincup with their riders, as an article of good faith in the present arrangement. "You've made a promise to those

men, San Saba, and you'h bound to make it good. But
I warn you, young man——!"

"Wait," responded San Saba evenly, his absent gaze
roving away. He was thinking bleakly of Rhoda Catlin, whose bewildering attitude he could not fathom.
He had seen his hat, hanging neglected at her saddle-
horn, and it had made something in him leap. Then
she had given him that bitter dig about his talking,
when she knew that it was the only thing that could
avert the fighting she so thoroughly deplored. He
shook his head.

For her part, as she helped round up the scattered
stock outside the fence, Rhoda felt like one under a
reprieve. She had not dared hope for the agreement
which had terminated this morning's hostilities; but
now that it had come, what did it mean? Was there
to be more, and bitterer, fighting?

Except one or two, the Spade men had turned back,
following Chris Mackey in a dour group toward
Feather Creek. Rhoda found it impossible to forget
them. There lingered in her mind the flashing glimpse
she had caught, a quarter-mile down the range fence,
of the stake-marked grave of Gene Rule. Her eye had
traced the fresh-heaped mound. Someone had hung
atop the stake the bleached white skull of a range
steer; and below that, in sardonic spirit, two leg bones
had been propped, crossed.

To her mind, it had been sinister in deadly promise, in no wise annulled by the sullen agreement to
arbitrate.

CHAPTER EIGHTEEN

THE DANGER TRAIL

DOGSOLDIER OLSEN sat on the top bar of the corral fence, which sagged under him alarmingly, and poked a large and blunt finger through a ragged hole in the brim of his Stetson, an expression of engrossment on his freckled face.

"What're you tryin' to do, Dogsoldieh—make it bigger?"

San Saba paused before the big fellow and studied quizzically the crinkled small eyes above the sandy stubble of a massive chin.

"Naw. Ay—Ay just tank about it, San Saba," Dogsoldier responded slowly. "Ay got dis hole over at the fence dis mornin'." He studied the hat minutely.

"Yeah." San Saba lazily scratched his sorrel head. "Theah was aplenty goin' on for awhile. I ain't figured out how come somebody didn't ride away belly-down across a horse."

"Somebody ban come near it, yah," Dogsoldier returned sententiously. "Ay tank the bullet what make this hole ban come from pretty close, too."

"Yes?"

"Ay tank it come from our side of the fence . . . Ay ban pretty close to you at the time."

San Saba knew what he was driving at. He had

no doubt Dogsoldier was telling him that Van Wagoner had tried to bushwhack him, and that the attempt had failed only by the narrowest margin.

"He ban not goin' to leave you alone, San Saba," Dogsoldier continued plainly, as the other threw rope on the pony he had selected. "Ay watch him pretty close dis mornin', but——"

San Saba shook his head. "Theah was a time, Dogsoldieh, when I'd have given a leg to lay hands on him. I guess I've changed, I reckon it's sense to stop trouble —not to look for more." He was surprised to find that he had changed to this extent during the past few weeks—or was it days?

Dogsoldier was stubborn, watching his foreman saddle up. "Van ban goin' be at dat schoolhouse. You look out for him. *He* don't want no sense." He hesitated. "Ay do somet'ing about it for you, San Saba, if you want."

San Saba slapped Olsen's big knee affectionately. "Lo'd love you, Dogsoldieh, no! I can shoot my own coyotes—if I have to."

But, riding away, he was more disturbed by Olsen's news, and his blunt offer, than otherwise. Dogsoldier's hat was the second to be punctured within a remarkably short time, as he believed, by Spade marksmen. It seemed reasonable now to believe that Van Wagoner had been behind the shots.

San Saba's resentment against the man was curiously impersonal. For Wagoner's venom toward himself he cared nothing. Wagoner's animosity was a force catapulted by chance into a situation requiring the utmost delicacy of handling.

It might well be that the man would try to ruin whatever truce San Saba was able to effect with the free-rangers. Chris Mackey did not want honorable adjustment with the free-lance stockmen. He did not, as near as San Saba could judge, believe such an adjustment possible; and he would instruct his minions accordingly.

"Yes, Mackey wants failure for me," he reflected soberly. "He's come heah from a land with much law, and he's found little. It's gone to his haid. He thinks theah's no law at all. But why he's left the law of decency behind, I can't see. It ce'tainly speaks bad for him."

Gazing across the broad prairie toward the swells of the Laramies, greening after the recent rains, he felt in his heart that the Englishman would do all in his power to smash the Casper parley and bring it to nought. It was a heavy thought, and one dark with storm, for San Saba could not let him do it.

The latter's determination to bring peace to the range had only strengthened with adversity. Circumstances had worked curiously to fortify his stand. The unpalatable example of Mackey in the rôle of plunderer and despot had been only a small part of the deciding influence.

San Saba had never, at heart, been on the side of the wire stringers. Any range policy which involved so strenuous a protest on the part of the men of the country could not be wholly right. In the beginning, the Tincup foreman had been somewhat quiescent. It was so easy to shrug the shoulders. And Colonel Purdy had given him a job—and what was more, of the kind he needed. Then, as though destined, the Catlins had appeared. Rhoda had walked into his ken once more, leading her pony; and it had changed everything.

So far as she was anything outside herself, Rhoda Catlin was, for him, the symbol of free-range rights. She humanized them and gave them meaning. Self-contained as she was, she was the spokesman for her brothers and their associates; her simple instinct was far more eloquent than their most determined outburst. Not that she insisted upon anything. What she wanted was untrammeled life; but she wanted safety too. A world in which women could find a place. It was incomprehensible that she should have to fight for these things.

It was this problem which occupied San Saba today. Only two days ago he had seen her in danger which had determined him to do something about it. Since then she had been imperiled twice over. Danger hung over her now. He remembered his feelings when she had ridden into that marrow-freezing situation at the range fence this morning. His very blood had congealed with fear for her. "And it was my own fault! I *asked* her to he'p me."

He rode toward Fetterman, across the prairie, and crossed the Platte above the Fort.

Belle Hammond's hotel was near the river. San Saba ground-anchored the bay outside the kitchen door and strolled inside. The cook shot him a glowering look reserved for cowboys who wandered in between meals with soft words and astonishing requests.

"Belle around?" San Saba asked.

The other relaxed. "Yeah. She's up switchin' blankets, guess."

San Saba went in search of her. He met Mrs. Hammond descending the stairs, and leaned over the rail, waiting for her to reach the bottom.

"Well, Lee! Fired?"

Belle Hammond was large and brusque, with a motherly solicitude under the surface. Her husband had been dead for five years, but she never lacked for men around, and treated one and all the same. She stopped, smiling, on the bottom step.

"No. Not yet. . . . Belle," he said abruptly, "d'you know Jess Catlin's outfit? Free-rangers—several brothehs?"

Belle mused. "Let's see—what was her name? Rose? No, Rhoda!" Her eyes twinkled. "Snubbed nose. Pretty brown hair. She's et a few meals with me; stayed over one night last fall. That who you mean?"

San Saba was unperturbed. "That's who. Belle, d'you like her?"

It seemed that Mrs. Hammond did. "She's a better man than some of these bull-voiced kids. Sturdier," she said firmly.

"Sho'. She is that. Well, will you do somethin' fo' her?"

"Can I ask you what?" Belle's tone was reserved.

San Saba did not smile. "Send somebody out to her —Jess is on the Lost Cabin—and ask her to come heah to the hotel for a week, two weeks? Say it's a visit. I'll pay."

"No," said Belle decisively.

"Now, look!" San Saba was frowning. "*I* don't expect to come neah her. It ain't that, Belle." He told her the situation on the range, which Belle knew; and added the dangers Rhoda had run, which Belle did not know. "I don't know what Jess can be thinkin' of. And *she* won't quit."

"Why, the poor child!" Belle broke in. She was won over easily. "She can't live like that. Send her to me. I'll make her stay!"

He shook his head. "She won't listen to me, Belle. Or to you either, if she knows I suggested it."

"Well, ride out there and tell one of Jess's boys. Say I want to see Rhoda, and leave the rest to me. You can do that, can't you?"

San Saba assented to this. He rode out of Fetterman toward Lost Cabin Creek. He had no idea where Rhoda might be, and wanted badly to see her.

"I hope never to see you again!" She had said that to him. Perhaps an hour later she would have withdrawn it. Nonetheless, something of the feeling of that moment would remain with her.

He swung wide of the Catlin camp. It would be as

awkward to meet the wrong rider as to meet Rhoda herself. His task was to avoid either.

San Saba was therefore all the more chagrined when he rode around a clump of willows five miles down the creek, and found the girl riding toward him at a distance of less than a furlong. It was too late to draw back. He met her with an expressionless face, waiting for her to speak.

"Why! . . . San Saba, what are you doing here?" she asked wonderingly.

His thoughts were in a turmoil. He saw suddenly that his plan must fail. If Rhoda was to receive word from Belle, even through another person, after having seen him, she would know he had brought it. Later she would perceive his hand behind Belle's proposal. He determined to throw the hotel idea into the discard, unless he could persuade her to it directly.

"Rhoda, I've been thinkin' about you. That's the truth."

Opposition arose behind her veiled gaze. He could feel it. Rhoda looked away quickly.

"That's . . . bad," she said finally. "I expect you know you've—no right to."

"Well, that's true too. But ma'am, somebody's got to." He saw that she believed he had come courting. "Look: this is no place for you. I know you'h not afraid, but—I can't stand it, even if Jess can! Rhoda, won't you go away for a while till this range a'gument is settled? It may be only fo' a few days."

"Where could I possibly go?" she breathed, as

though to herself. Then she stiffened. "I'll think about it," she added briefly.

"No! Ma'am, you'll think it oveh, an' then fo'get it! Won't you please get out from undeh? Rhoda—I *mean* it!" His face darkened with blood, but his tone was staunch.

She cooled perceptibly, her horse backing a step to the tightened rein. "Yes? I daresay you do. . . ." She looked at him oddly.

"Ma'am—you'h not safe! These men are unbridled, wild for fight. You know how they are when they let themselves go. If one of them sta'ts afteh you——!"

"I know—what they are," she responded, coloring. "I think I can take care of myself."

"But you can't! You'll never know! I tell you——" He stopped as though shot, watching her nodding head. He was "doing nothing except talk" again! "Ma'am," he bit off, "I shouldn't talk to you. You won't listen. . . . Well, you won't have to much longeh! I'm goin' to do somethin'!"

"What are you going to do?" she demanded sharply.

"I'm goin' to take you somewheah safe myse'f— and you'll go!"

The blood drained away from her cheeks. "No, you'll not! I never dreamed *you'd* be the—man to 'start after' me!" Her tone was scathing.

San Saba's jaws clamped. "Neve'theless, I will be! An' right now! Rhoda——" He pressed the bay forward as he spoke. She cut him off:

"Stay where you are!"

He paid no attention to it. His eyes burned with decisive mastery as he came on, his features set.

Rhoda half-pulled her pony around; then quickly turned back. Her gun was in her hand now.

"Stop!"

He laughed harshly.

"San Saba—you force me——!" she gasped.

The gun cracked. The bay sprang forward under him with a snorting scream. San Saba slid out of the saddle, bringing up on his knees just as the horse fell prostrate, dead where it landed. He turned with a face of fury.

"Why did you do that?" he blazed.

"I——" she began. Her face was as white as a sheet.

"San Saba, I *had* to!" she ejaculated in muffled tones. "You'll not take me—anywhere!"

She had the presence of mind to back her pony away as he came toward her. He said no more, his gaze intent. When he made a spring, she jammed her spurs into the *palomino* and burst running from the spot, shaking with anger and mortification; anger at San Saba for his presumption, chagrin that she should have shot the horse.

When she looked back, minutes later, he was still standing where he had been, staring after her.

CHAPTER NINETEEN

HOW TO LIVE

R HODA had been on her way to Fetterman when she met San Saba. She was oblivious of the passing minutes as the *palomino* settled to a road gait and went steadily on. Never had she been imbued with a greater sense of outrage. She felt misused and unfortunate, and she could not shake off her frenzy of indignation.

For two days she had wavered miserably between championing and disapproval of San Saba. On the day of Glen's death she had been numb and stricken under a double blow. It had seemed to her that San Saba's inaction overshadowed even the wolfish depravity of the Spade men. Mercifully for San Saba, the occurrences of the next night at Chiles and Packer's Platte camp had wrought his subtle reinstatement in her heart. During the battle at the drift fence she had felt closer to him than she had ever been.

But now! Her cheeks dyed as she relived the moments with him. He had been insufferable—telling her that he intended to take her somewhere away, as if she were a child! The nerve of him! Her resistance to his overbearing advances had been instinctive. Never had she felt more certain that she could take care of herself than at that moment; and she had proved it, she hoped, so decisively that he would never question her ability again.

Let him go his way for good and all! Rhoda would have no more of his magisterial dominance. She recognized with sudden repugnance his arrogant presumption toward all men and all things. As though the range fence, and the range war itself, belonged to him —as though *she* were his girl, his possession!

She entered the lower end of Fetterman's single street, mastered by an odd fluttering of nerves that had nothing to do with outside influences. So preoccupied was she as she rode toward Marcus's general store that she failed to note the air of tenseness in the town.

Few people were in the street. She saw several faces at doors—and one man in the middle of the road, coming this way, as though prowling. His raking glance searched the alleys and doors on either side. Then, a hundred yards behind him, another man sauntered into the open. The first man whirled. They stared at each other, silent, a vulpine grace in either tensed figure. Each began to walk toward the other.

Rhoda pulled the *palomino* around sharply, suddenly aware of what was happening. She pressed back toward the side of the street and turned into a wide alley, trembling. It was only by accident that she found herself alongside Hammond's hotel.

Belle was standing on the steps at the side door, glancing sharply.

"Rhoda Catlin?" she exclaimed. "Get down, honey, and come in here. I want to see you!"

Rhoda dismounted and trailed the rein, and then stepped forward mechanically, glad to see and hear another woman.

"I thought you'd come—you did it quick enough, Lord knows!" Belle was scanning her features shrewdly.

Rhoda paused. "Mrs. Hammond, I . . . What do you mean?" she queried. She started nervously as several banging explosions sounded from the street.

"Come on in here! Hurry up!" Belle commanded in a high, easy tone, holding the door. "Why, you got my message, didn't you?" she asked, as Rhoda stepped in.

They were in a large, quiet hall.

"I got no message," Rhoda countered.

Belle led her to the empty dining-room and seated her in a chair. "What? Didn't that no-'ccount, worthless . . . Well, honey, I sent one! I expect you to stay with me for a few days. You might have brought your nightie. . . . No back-chat, now! Don't you know it's no place for you, out there on some crick, with what's going on?" She smoothed the dress over her ample lap and began to abuse Rhoda amiably. "That's no way for a self-respecting girl to live. I won't have it!"

Rhoda started up as the import of this surprising proposal sank home. "Mrs. Hammond——"

"Just Belle, honey."

"—I appreciate your thinking of me, I honestly do; but I can take care of myself," Rhoda fought on, her emotions tumbling. "I—I can't possibly stay. And——"

"Nonsense!" Belle said explosively.

"—what is more, I don't believe it is your idea at all!"

"Why! What do you mean?" Belle was nonplussed. "Whose idea is it, then?"

"San—Saba Lee's!" Rhoda got out, with heightened color. "He came to you—I am sure of it—and you sent him. . . . *Oh!*" she ejaculated, as the full force of the plan came to her. Had she not been forewarned by the meeting with San Saba, she might almost certainly have accepted Belle Hammond's invitation. She gasped at the abyss which would have been thus opened beneath her feet. A fresh wave of anger swept her at the man's effrontery.

"I don't understand you!" Belle said shortly, her brows drawn down. "Is there anything——" She changed this swiftly; "did you meet this Lee somewhere, Rhoda?"

"Yes!"

"And did he mention my hotel—or my name?" Belle asked carefully. She could have wrung San Saba's neck for blundering.

"N-no. . . . He didn't have to." The words came rushing out now: "He said that *he* was going to take me—somewhere safe! He must have been thinking —must have known—about you! *He* said that 'some-

body had to think about me'! He had the sense not
to mention you—I was on my way to the store—and
you found me by accident. But I can see it now! It
was *his* idea—and he came to you—and then I fell
over him and spoiled it!"

Belle was fainly incensed. "Well! It was his idea, if
you'll have it so! And then what, lady?"

Rhoda's countenance was distraught. "I won't have
it! Do you hear? I won't!" She stamped her foot.
Tears of mortification hung on her lashes. "I despise
him! I'd tear him out of my thoughts if I could! How
any man can . . . Oh—I beg your pardon!" she broke
off; and putting her hands on Belle Hammond's capable shoulders, she bowed her head and burst into
a fit of weeping.

"There, there, honey!" Belle consoled her, chang-
ing front instantly, patting her back gently. "Let it
go! No man's worth it!" She crooned for minutes,
while the girl gradually calmed.

"I mean it," Rhoda said quietly at last. She was
still moved to frozen anger. "I wish I might forget
him entirely! He'll not leave me alone. He's always
there, driving me to distraction! I—I'll have nothing
to do with his fears and hopes! I *can't* stay!"

Belle's sympathies were large. "You're just dead
right, honey! Make him keep his distance. You just
go on and live the way you want to—and damn them
all! And if there's ever anything Aunt Belle can do
for you, you just sing out!"

So it turned out better than Rhoda had dared expect; although, riding home an hour later, bulwarked by Belle Hammond's approval, the remembrance of her own vehemence frightened her. She marshaled every reason she possessed for the rejection of San Saba from her sacred confidence.

There was one score that she had held against him since before Glen's death—doubt of his essential sincerity; his clinging to his position, his refusal to explain. *Why* did he not give up his foremanship and throw in with the free-rangers, unless he was playing a deeper game?

He was not cowardly. She realized now that it took greater courage for endless conciliation than for fighting. Was he working for the defeat of free-range rights? Rhoda could not swear whether he did right or wrong, noble or evil; but she sensed in his course a basic betrayal that called forth all her resentment.

She reached the camp on the Lost Cabin in time to cook supper for her men, who rode in dusty and silent at the last minute. She studied Smoke Chaloner and Red, wondering whether San Saba had come to one of them for a horse. Billy glowered at her like a man with a biting grievance. It was not until the meal was over, however, that he began his inevitable ill-natured tirade.

"Where was you this afternoon?" he demanded as they gathered the dishes up. He had seen her ride in late.

"I went to Fetterman for thread."

"Yeah. I know you!" He snorted.

"Thread! You went some'eres to meet San Saba Lee!"

Rhoda gasped: "Billy!"

"Leave 'er alone, you!" Jess growled.

Billy whirled on him. "Why should I? *You* know there's somethin' between them two! Wasn't Lee over here the day Glen was plugged? What fer? Chasin' her—that's what!"

"Aw——" Jess demurred.

"Wal, all right! But jest the same, a fool could tell! I *tole* you the reason Lee didn't lift a hand that day! He shore did later—bangin' me over the head in Fetterman! An' you see him ridin' away from town with them fellers, didn't you? How'd that set with you?"

"Whut's that got to do with Rho'?" Jess countered stolidly.

"Plenty!" Billy blazed. "*She* knows how rotten he is —but didn't she stick up fer him at that meetin' on the Platte? I heard 'bout her hangin' onto his hat! An' later she was talkin' to him at the range fence too! Wasn't he the first one out there to 'er?"

Rhoda had held her peace as long as she was able. Now she retorted hotly: "It's none of your business, Billy Catlin! I know what I'm doing! Didn't we stop the fighting? What do you suppose my object was?"

"I guess you know, orright—livin' the way yo're doin'!" Billy snapped scathingly. "You can't fool me! It was him you was thinkin' about at that fence, not us! If you have to go fallin' in love with a dog like that——!"

"He is not a dog! And he isn't rotten!" she flared, oblivious of Billy's glare and Jess's gruff remonstrance. "He is a brave man, doing what he can! And as for my falling in love with him . . . !" She mustered all the scorn she could toward the suggestion: "You're crazy!"

Billy was shouting now: "So you say—you little slut!" His face was flaming. *"Was* you with him this afternoon, or wasn't you? Answer me that!"

Rhoda was struck dumb. With the inevitability of that question, something welled up in her that was foreign to her experience—a fierce, reckless indifference. She *had* been with San Saba; and accidental as it had been, she was glad of it. She knew now. She loved him while she stood up for him against all comers; she had loved him this afternoon, in the midst of her wild huff. *She had loved him all along!* For hours—for days—she had fought against it until she was exhausted. She might as well give up. If she could not keep the truth away from Billy, how could she keep it from herself?

"Yes," she said quietly, "I was with him." Not for anything, now, would she confess that she had shot San Saba's horse to get away from him.

Billy was boiling with excited rage.

"I told you!" he yelled at Jess. "That hydrophoby skunk sneakin' around Rho' all the time! Whut're you goin' to do?" He swung on Rhoda: "Damn you, girl, sister or not, if you so much as look cross-eyed at that bird again, I'll drop him in his tracks!"

"*Hyar!*" Jess's tone was a blare of wrath. "You haul yore long nose outa this pronto, feller, an' take it away from hyar! Git!" Taking a stride forward, he stared Billy down and watched him stalk away in a quaking tumult. Then he turned.

He was surprisingly gentle as he laid a hard hand on Rhoda's shoulder. "I reckon it's hell all around, Rho'," he said heavily; "but as long as I'm hyar, you'll live how you want. Only—use all the brains you've got, girl; and then pray fer more." He patted her reassuringly.

Rhoda was too astonished at the revolution within herself to take note of the change in Jess. As she went blindly on with the dishes, choking back to something like calm, she concluded with a forlorn dejection that she did not know how to live. But she would not give up trying.

CHAPTER TWENTY

SINGLE-HANDED

TEN minutes after Rhoda had left him, San Saba had not yet succeeded in freeing his saddle from the dead bay. The latigo was caught under the animal's bulk. San Saba heaved and sawed with discouraging results.

He swung up sharply, red-faced, hearing hoofs pound behind him. Had Rhoda come back?

She had not. It was Smoke Chaloner, imperturbable astride a sleepy-eyed roan with straw mane. The middle-aged puncher was studying the tell-tale bullet hole in the bay's chest. His eyes swung to San Saba, hardening.

"Whar'd she go to?" he demanded brusquely.

San Saba knew instantly who he meant. "That's more than I can say, Chaloneh. She made sho' I didn't follow."

Smoke's flinty gaze seemed quizzical. He understood. "D'you s'pose you would've done it if you could, Lee?"

San Saba flared shortly: "Ce'tainly I would! What are *you* doin', if not that?"

Smoke considered. "S'pose I was to ask you why, Lee?" he pressed on dryly.

San Saba had turned back to the bay. He jerked an

irritated look over his shoulder. "If you must know, I was goin' to take her somewheah out of this mess. It's no place fo' her." His tone was impatient.

"Whar, fer instance?" Smoke persisted.

San Saba straightened. "Why—Belle Hammond's hotel, Chaloneh, an' be damned to you!" His level gaze met the other's briefly. "I expect somebody else *can* worry about the girl, when you'h busy?"

Chaloner said nothing for several minutes, musing. "She went on to'rds Fetterman, didn't she?" he resumed at last.

"Yes!" San Saba grunted, rather than spoke the word. He succeeded in releasing his saddle.

"Wal, in that case . . ." Smoke debated with himself, "if you'll jest set awhile, I'll git you a hoss to ride."

San Saba turned immediately, his eyes kinder. "Why, then I will," he agreed. "An' Chaloneh, I don't think she'll come to any harm from eitheh you or me. She can stand alone."

Smoke grunted in reply. He swung the roan and cantered away without looking back. Half-an-hour later he returned with a handsome dun mare.

Throwing his saddle on the pony, San Saba glanced ruefully at the Pitchfork brand on the animal's flank. That would look swell to his enemies, he thought. Still it was better than walking.

"I'm obliged, Chaloneh," he acknowledged the favor.

Smoke waved a hand. So they parted.

San Saba was thinking, as he headed for the Tincup,

that he had seen his last of Rhoda Catlin. After his fool play she would avoid him as she would a plague, and probably she was thoroughly justified. It struck him with a touch of grimness that whatever trouble might come to him from the horse he rode must remain his last memento from that girl.

Colonel Purdy accosted him as he was swinging the sweat-stained saddle off the trim dun. There was something on the older man's mind. His eye sharpened as he noted the mare's brand. San Saba heard him snort softly. He made no direct reference to the pony, however.

"I don't know why we didn't stay right theah and fix that fence this mo'ning, San Saba," he began half-querulously. "I keep thinking about that. It's a hole, and I might just as well not have any fence. My stock——"

San Saba returned to work-a-day affairs with a wrench. "Think how it would have looked, Kunnel Dick!" he urged, frowning. "We wo'ked hard to win those boys oveh. Then if we'd gone right at the fence and built it back up undeh their noses, they'd be all ready to tear the Caspeh schoolhouse down at the drop of the hat."

"Well, boy, that's just it!" exclaimed the Colonel quickly. "They will anyway! . . . Look at it this way: We didn't offeh them a thing, and we ain't going to! They won't get anything from me that'll be wo'th havin'. An' that'll leave them right wheah they were.

. . . I am not goin' to tear down my fence to suit them, an' that is final! Will they take any less?"

San Saba was studious of manner. "I think they will, suh; an' I think you will too! Those boys showed real forbearance, and they deserve credit. . . . You ain't playin' faih, Kunnel Dick. We decided we'd all cool off for a couple days."

Colonel Purdy grunted: "D'you think anybody's goin' to be cooled off when we get to Casteh, San Saba? Because I don't! We'll have trouble theah! What pleases me is that it'll end in noise, an' no more. . . . I begin to think you'h shrewder than I knew, givin' those men time to get used to the idea of that fence. By tomorro' night they'll be broke to lead, and it's a good thing. They won't get any biggah favor from me!"

San Saba stared at him piercingly.

"I would expect that kind of talk from Christ'pher Mackey, suh. To heah you say it makes me wondeh if I've mistaken my man."

The Colonel's voice rose: "What d'you mean by that, you young——?"

"I mean this!" San Saba broke in sharply. "In Tennessee you've been used to havin' black slaves thank you for simple justice! In Wyomin' theah are no slaves; nor do they know the care and treatment of tyrants—even such a reasonable one," he added gently, "as you are."

He turned and walked toward the saddle-shed shamblingly with his burden.

"Whateveh it is, you young scoundrel, they are goin'
to feel the hand of one—if that is what you call it!"
Colonel Purdy shouted after him, scarlet-faced.

Rolling a cigarette in the shadow of the saddle-shed
with steady hands, San Saba was amazed at the lan-
guage he had used on his employer. That Colonel
Purdy should countenance it was still more astound-
ing. San Saba had been fired in his young and careless
days for less. That he was not now made him easier
in his mind. To him this brief flare, occasioned by
his unexplained use of a horse bearing a free-range
brand, meant that Colonel Dick was serving notice
on him. He must attack the range knot and solve it
single-handed and alone. Was there anyone at all—
except Rhoda, who had rejected him—who honestly
hoped for the avoidance of range war? Not one person of influence did he know on whom he could count
to stand by him unreservedly.

It did not discourage him. Rather he felt in himself
the slow surge and development of anger, a stubborn,
inexorable determination.

He was well aware of the potential peril in the gathering that would crowd into the little Casper schoolhouse tomorrow night. Suspicion of hidden guns would
be rife. Perhaps a smuggled Colt or two would appear.
It was a long chance for any of them to take; but
unless some faction cautiously backed out of the parley at the last minute, it must be taken.

He knew to a nicety that the Casper parley must
be final. Whichever way the range fortune went, there

must lie the future road for them all. If the meeting was a failure, then it was war, and bitter war. The lives already lost in the range dispute would be but a beginning to a terrible and bloody struggle, in which free-ranger and barb-wire advocate must stand opposed to the last.

The very territory itself would be disrupted. The Catlins and others of his friends would overnight become hostile strangers to San Saba and his kind. Rhoda Catlin, whom he had already lost, would be a girl he had once known, but who, for him, was henceforth as good as dead.

CHAPTER TWENTY-ONE

AT CASPER SCHOOLHOUSE

HONESTY is the best policy," was the legend that had been painstakingly traced by some childish hand across the painted wooden blackboard on the wall of the Casper schoolroom in letters a foot high. By the earnest, sober look in their faces, it was evident that this was the policy that was to be followed by the group of big, broad-shouldered, per-spiring men who had gathered here tonight, dwarfing the little room.

They said little, gazing at one another with cool and formal decorum; for the full list of disputants had not yet congregated. The swinging lantern in the center of the room had been lit, although not all the light had died out in the sky outside.

Out there, saddle horses stood at the rails along either side of the schoolhouse, cartridge belts and holstered forty-fives hanging from nearly every saddle-horn. Each group of ponies was presided over by an indolent but watchful man who had not removed his gun.

Diagonally across the street four more men stood in a group on the porch of the general store. Farther along, the stage hotel was notable for the bull-whack-ers, tin-horns, stage passengers and others who stared up the street toward the school with speculative interest. On both sides of the street the saloons were booming, the lighted windows flooding the dusty ground outside. An air of taut expectancy held the little town.

Up from the river towards the schoolhouse in the afterglow rode a silent cavalcade who drew rein at the hitching-rack. A heavy, spur-jingling step sounded at the door. "Who's that?" Bitter Creek demanded.

"Purdy's outfit," one of the horse-guards answered.

Bitter Creek grunted. " 'Bout time. Go down an' tell the Spade bunch we're all here, huh?" he suggested to Len Bain. "They're in Jack McGowan's."

Len sauntered away. Bitter Creek, in the door, backed aside as Colonel Purdy, San Saba, Dogsoldier Olsen, Pink Robinette and two other cowboys stamped in. Brief nods were exchanged under the lantern with the free-range men gathered around Jess Catlin and Hank Chiles. Then all waited stiffly for the Spade boys to appear.

Most of the children's benches had been stacked out of the way. Several larger benches, and the teacher's desk, were arranged in the form of a rectangle. Only Bandy Packer, Old Blue, with his slung arm, and one or two more had taken seats, the rest remaining on their feet.

Chris Mackey came striding in authoritatively with Arapahoe Jones. Three cowboys accompanied them. Mackey, Colonel Purdy, Jess Catlin and other principals seated themselves with throat-clearing deliberation. Punchers gathered in a standing circle under the lantern.

"Wal, Purdy?" Jess began shortly. "You suggested this." He glanced around. "I take it we're most all hyar."

Colonel Dick's brows rose, his gaze wandering to San Saba. Then he recollected himself. "Boys," he said, "let's get this heah straight an' plain. What *is* it you-all have got against the ba'bed-wire? Tell me that, now."

Restlessness imbued nearly everyone as the question was put.

Packer spoke up: "Why, hell! You fellers've cut off the trail to the railroad—onless we drive more'n a hunderd miles plumb around! What else do we need ag'inst it?"

"Yes? Well, but . . . Hm'm." The Colonel put up a hand as Chris Mackey was about to speak. "That's a reasonable a'gument. I don't know just what to . . . But now!" he added, in the tone of discovery; "stand up heah, you San Saba! Dammit, man; you got me into this——!"

San Saba brushed forward. "Boys," he addressed them, "I more or less high-pressured this meetin'. Eve'y one of you deserve thanks for showin' up. The question we're thrashin' out is pretty scrambled, an' we'll save time an' sorrow by siftin' it good an' thoro'. I've got a plan I propose to put; but let's understand each other first."

He looked around. He was thinking fast, now. Van

Wagoner had not put in an appearance, and the omission struck him as dubious.

"We'll just see what we can agree on," he continued quietly. "Is it goin' to be fair play all around?"

Nods, grunts, murmurs of "Shore," "Whut're we here fer?" and the like until Arapahoe Jones put in: "Come off, Lee!" His tone was scornful.

San Saba appeared surprised. "Why! Aren't you fello's fixin' to meet the rest of us half-way? How about it, Mist' Mackey?"

Scowling at his foreman, who had brought down on him this direct question, Chris Mackey conceded that he was.

San Saba was relieved. "Sho' . . . Well now, let's go back to Kunnel Dick's point." He faced the free-rangers. "What have you boys got against the fence —aside from it cuttin' you off from the south—if anythin'?"

Growls and ominous looks met this. As Bandy Packer was clearing his throat, Bitter Creek leaned forward and spoke:

"Why, it's too plumb advanced for us, San Saba. *You* know whut fence means! It means dirt farmers, an' choppin' the land up! Picayune pop'lation, an' too much gov'ment! Them rotten 'law an' order' polyticians are worse than straight-up man rule. That's what we've got ag'in fencin'!"

Bitter Creek's companions grinned and nodded firmly, convinced.

"That's sense, Bittah Creek. Let's look at it a minute. You say the fence means dirt farmers, but you know better than that. Farmin' takes water. Except for the Platte, theah's just about enough water heah for the cows—an' the cows are already heah. How does that leave any to spare for a flock of cabbages?"

"That's right," Jess Catlin admitted cautiously.

"An' what's more—if we fence the graze, wheah *is* the little farmer?" San Saba pursued. "He's out! . . . In fact, I'd say free-rangin' is wo'se for them than fencin'. You leave the land to be squatted on, if theah's any done."

Many were listening closely, caught. On Chris Mackey's thin red face, however, was an expression of contempt.

"Just to show you," San Saba began afresh; "take this place we're in right now. A schoolhouse! That means youngstehs, mo' population growin' up—our kind of folks."

"Our kind of fool hoe men!" Hank Chiles put in forcibly. "Feller, d'you know there's two-three dozen farmers, west of here 'long the creeks, growin' stuff right now?"

"Along the rivah—yes, suh; Gene Morgan's the biggest of 'em," San Saba caught him up. "Gene's a fine man too. An' d'you know what Gene's raisin'? Alfalfa grass! It's that new stuff from back East a ways— two, three crops a season—and it's for cows! You'll be buyin' that stuff from him, Hank——"

"I shore will if I get stuck down here behind a fence in the dry season!" Chiles rejoined gruffly.

"Well—yes—but Hank, look! Right now theah's a petition circulatin' east of heah—an' in Montana an' Colorado—an' goin' straight to Washington. What for? Askin' the gov'ment to open a cattle trail from Texas to this country, an' keepin' it from bein' closed off! An' why, Hank? Because of ba'bed-wire! I tell you the stuff is comin' to this country as sure as it came to Kansas, an' down into Texas itself——"

Outside, at this juncture, sounded exuberant shots above a lugubrious cowboy croon. A moment later voices arose at the schoolhouse door.

"You ban take off dat gun, Wagoner! Else, you don't come in here, yah!"

"If you don't git outa my way, squarehead, I'll blast you out of it!" Van Wagoner's half-intoxicated truculence was distinguishable above O'Malley's seconding: "Push 'im over, Van. . . . Here! Lemme at 'im!"

Slight scuffling sounded, and then a grunting thud, followed by a flood of infuriated blasphemy.

The gathered men inside the building looked at one another. Arapahoe Jones stumbled up and began to press through the circle. "Lemme out there! I'll damper them two!"

Crowding past San Saba, Arapahoe trod his feet soundly. San Saba braced himself, and with a panther-like jolt, thrust Jones half across the room. He knew instantly what was afoot. The Spade men were attempting a concerted disruption of the proceedings, and Arapahoe was acting his appointed part.

The latter reeled, cursing. With a countenance of

thunder he whirled on San Saba. It was a tense moment. Recriminations sounded outside; violence threatened here under the lantern.

It was Billy Catlin who snatched at Arapahoe's arm as his hand slid under his waistcoat. Jones' six-gun wavered, glinting, in the yellow light. Jess wrenched it away and thrust between them.

"Gun, eh?" he growled wrathfully.

"Gimme that hog-leg!" Arapahoe broke out belligerently. He made a grab, but many hands were there to intercept him.

Suddenly, at the door, Dogsoldier exploded into action, kicking and cuffing. A shot roared, thwacking the boards outside; Olsen bellowed; then sounded the swearing retreat of Wagoner and O'Malley.

Hank Chiles forced Arapahoe back and demanded: "D'you wanto stay here or go outside with your playmates, you coyote?"

"Put 'im out!"

"Make 'im eat that gun!"

"Wait, now—hold everythin'!" Bandy Packer, stocky, hard and calm, waved an arm. "Throw that Colt outside!" It was done with dispatch. Pack's growl at Jones made the windows rattle: "Si'down!" He turned to San Saba: "Lee, you've got somethin' to spill. Git to it!"

Jess, Colonel Purdy and others jerked nods. Men crowded closer.

"Ve'y well. It's this," San Saba began. "Will you

boys be satisfied with a passage south through the
fence range—if you get it?"

Exclamations arose, in the midst of which, despite
his disciplining, Arapahoe Jones said violently: *"If
you git it!"*

"Go on, Lee," Jess commanded.

Chris Mackey was staring at San Saba with wrath;
Colonel Dick with astonished suspicion.

"What I propose," San Saba went on firmly, "is a
half-mile lane down the valley between the Spade an'
the Tincup. That'll give us fence an' it'll give you
passage—it's meetin' you more than half-way."

Pin-drop silence followed, in the midst of which
Chris Mackey scraped his feet.

"No, sir!" he declared vehemently, furiously. "Not
a foot of my range!—Not unless you take half-a-mile
of Tincup land!"

Colonel Purdy's face congested. "Why, damn you,
Mackey! Not that I agree with this; but you——!"

"Hold up!" San Saba gripped them with a manner
of chilled steel. He challenged Jess and Packer: "Does
that suit you—this lane?"

"Why——" Jess began, rubbing his jaw.

Packer and Hank Chiles appeared uncertain, but
not flatly dissenting. Others plainly debated with themselves.

"Hang it, San Saba! I tell you——" Colonel Purdy
opened afresh.

"Now!" the Tincup foreman warned. He went on:
"It's easy done. A quarter-mile off each ranch—in

twenty mile strips. It won't be nothin'! But it'll be eve'ything to these boys heah!"

"*No!*" Chris Mackey thundered.

A battery of stares was turned on him. He faced them unmoved. His law was set, his eyes sharp.

San Saba's patience was inexhaustible: "Mackey, why *don't* you want a lane?"

The Spade manager blustered: "Why should I give these wolves anything? . . . It means two fences, for one thing! Will *they* pay for the other one?" He indicated the free-rangers contemptuously.

Snorts met his stubborn refusal; glares of enmity.

"Blast you, Mackey——!"

"Kunnel Dick, can *you* see youh way clear to agreein' to this?" San Saba persisted.

"Wal! I guess I've got to!" the Colonel responded shortly. "But *I* ain't been the point of this a'gument! You talk to Mackey!"

A majority seemed with San Saba now, or wavering.

"Mackey," he said pointedly, "did I heah you say somethin' about comin' half-way in this?"

Mackey exploded in virulent anger. "*No!* Curse you, Lee; you tricked and trapped me in that! I'll agree to nothing! Not a foot of my range! I've got England to consult in these matters! I wash my hands of the whole proposition!"

"Wagh-h! Le's clean up on this—then go fer the fences!" Billy Catlin bawled. The schoolroom thundered hollowly to the words.

Jess shoved Billy back before anyone had made a

move. He stood at his full height and bent his eagle's gaze on Mackey.

"Hyar we are ag'in!" he rumbled. "Jest nowhar . . . I reckon we knowed what to expect of you big fellers! Bred stock, an' fence wire! Fresh milk an' chicken eggs! Alfalfar an' beef-eatin' ramrods! Why, hell's fire——!"

"Catlin, look!" San Saba thrust in, as Mackey's men grouped around him, muttering darkly. He got no further.

"Go wan!" Jess fired back. "This hyar's done! You, Lee; I know you didn't——"

He was cut off by Arapahoe Jones' vigorous thrust. Billy Catlin promptly countered with a swinging blow to the latter's jaw. Outcry arose, and the men milled, moved by differing motives at first, but swinging into the melee with enthusiasm. Shouts rang out, calls, threats, warnings. Arms rose and fell, fists pummeling. In a moment the Casper schoolhouse was converted into the scene of a free-for-all.

San Saba thought first of Colonel Purdy, who had no place in such a fracas. Heads were likely to be broken here. Colonel Dick had lost his hat already; his graying head shone across the mass of struggling men. Toward it the Texan began to strive, intent upon his employer's protection.

A flailing fist struck the base of the hanging lantern. It swung once in a lurid arc and then blinked out.

The room instantly seemed to become a shambles. No one was any longer certain who anyone else was, but the blows did not cease. They fell like rain, like hail, like thunderbolts, indiscriminately. A stack of piled benches came down with a crash, adding to the confusion.

The cries turned to groans and gasps. Thuds and thumps sounded, and the scrape of heavy bodies. Nearly everyone was down now, those underneath fighting for simple survival.

San Saba lost track of Colonel Dick. He contented himself with pulling man after man off the heap, and sending them reeling toward the door.

At last the fighting knot bade fair to resolve itself. Figures staggered out the door: the footsteps of escaping men pounded away; ejaculations, and scuffling, lessened. San Saba stood back and struck a match on his lifted thigh. It flickered while he relit the lantern.

Five men remained in the little room. Colonel Dick half-staggered against the wall, his nose bleeding, an expression of comical ferocity in his eyes.

Joe Brush lay on the floor, groaning. Dogsoldier straightened him out and sent him spinning away. Joe stumbled through the door and tumbled headlong. It left, besides the Swede, Colonel Purdy and San Saba, Pink Robinette half-sitting on the boards near the door in a dazed condition.

"That settles that!" Colonel Dick got out wrathfully, with a reproachful stab of eyes at San Saba.

"Yes—I reckon that closes the case!" San Saba conceded slowly, wiping his brow to conceal his twinge of sickening discouragement. "Thank God theah wasn't any guns in this! . . . Not but what theah will be, come daylight. In the meantime, we might's well straighten up a bit heah, and hit for the Tincup."

But all that he could think of, as they went about the commonplace anticlimax to the free-for-all, was the accusative eyes of Rhoda Catlin, whom he had once more failed.

CHAPTER TWENTY-TWO

REVENGE IS SWEET

RETIRING to McGowan's saloon after their repulse by Dogsoldier Olsen, Van Wagoner and Tex O'Malley solaced themselves with copious libations of whisky. Accurately identified by townsfolk, they were left to themselves under the disgruntled stare of the bartender. The schoolhouse meeting was going on, after their abortive attempt to wreck it; but they were indifferent.

"Hell with it!" Wagoner growled, in an ugly mood. " 'Rapahoe Jones is in there, with Mackey. Why didn' he get goin'?"

"Right!" Tex grunted, helping himself to another glass. "Let 'em work too!"

They heard the uproar at the schoolhouse as the parley broke up in violence. Having no means of determining the outcome, they thought that Jones and his companions had routed the free-rangers. They gazed at one another, grinning; finally O'Malley walked to the door. He could see nothing in the gloom.

"They're tumblin' outa there in a hurry—that's a fact!" he exulted, probing the darkness.

He saw shadowy figures racing for the horse-racks, and heard the heavy pound of hoofs. Then his grin faded. "Cripes——!" He turned back to the bar with flashing face. "Van, I'd swear I saw Mackey rip past, hell-fer-leather! . . . Didn't he ride a paint hoss?"

Wagoner nodded. They stared at each other questioningly.

"Mebbe we better git up there!" O'Malley bit out. "If them free-grazers fort up in that school-house——!" He lifted the six-guns at his hips, settling the belts more firmly.

Men ran past the door of the saloon, calling hoarsely. Then Arapahoe Jones and Denny Jackson stamped into the bar with thunderous faces. The Spade foreman had an angry bruise on his prominent cheek-bone, and one of his ears bled from a scratch.

"What's goin' on?" O'Malley demanded instantly.

"Rough-house," Arapahoe flung back, shooting a wicked stare. "What'd you think it was—from here?" he added bitingly.

Wagoner ignored the sarcasm. "Where's the boys, Jones?"

Arapahoe waved a hand disgustedly. "Flew the coop!" The explosive words sounded cavernous with scorn. Arapahoe poured himself a slug, and slid the bottle to Denny.

Wagoner and O'Malley were still taut with astonishment. "What about Mackey?" the former persisted, his manner incredulous.

"Aw, look——" Jones began grudgingly; "I started a battle, see? Ever'body into it! It was damned rough, feller, an' don't you fergit it! We started in the school, an' wound up outside! Nobody knowed who anybody was. It jest ended with kicks. . . . Mackey dusted."

He stared into his glass broodingly, and began afresh, belligerently: "What's a matter with you two, anyway? Where in hell was you when things started to pop?"

Wagoner stared back defiantly. "We was there!" he countered, bristling.

"The hell you was! You quit cold!"

"What if we did? You had a gun! If you'd let us in there in the first place, we could've done somethin'!"

"Yas—an' we'd do somethin' now, if we c'd find out what!" O'Malley broke in truculently. "You an' Mackey, an' yore damn mystery! . . . Where's Catlin an' Packer an' that bunch?"

"They're down in the River Bend, lickin' their sore spots," Denny Jackson inserted. "We know where to find them, orright!"

The undertone that ran through the gathering of free-rangers at the River Bend saloon a hundred yards away was like the angry buzzing of bees.

"Wal, I guess them fellers've stalled us 'bout long 'nough!" Len Bain muttered portentously, gazing at the others.

"You tell 'em! Here we are; only set back a few

from where we started from!" Hank Chiles seconded grimly.

"Bob-wire lane!" Billy Catlin burst out contemptuously. "They'll shore hang theirselves with wire yet! . . . We could've expected that from Lee!"

"Wal," Jess put in more temperately, "it would give us some of what we wanted. Lee was *tryin'* to do the right thing——"

"But they ain't give us no lane yet!" Packer interrupted. "An' they won't! 'Rapahoe said——"

He was cut off by the outburst of argumentative voices. Casper habitues, sympathetic to the free-range cause, joined in. Behind the group, the bartender was shuffling the glasses, listening with long ears.

Jess beat down the racket. "You'all heard Purdy agree to a lane!" he pointed out. "It's you blame bull-dozers that's got us all in an uproar! If you go hellin' off ag'in, you'll go by yoreself—because I won't!" He stared piercingly for a moment, and then pushed through the circle, stalking to the far end of the bar.

"Now look, Jess!" Hank Chiles began, following him. Bandy Packer went also, along with Smoke Chaloner, Old Blue and others.

The remaining free-rangers stared after them resentfully. Then, lowering his voice, Len Bain said forcefully:

" 'Rapahoe an' Jackson an' one-two others went into McGowan's place. I seen 'em. They're up there yet."

Billy's head jerked around. "Jones? . . . Is *Lee* up there?" He clipped the queries off.

"Didn' see 'im. . . . Shall we go up there an' tromp on 'em?"

"Wal, I guess!" Joe Brush breathed harshly. Accustomed to going unarmed except for his rifle, tonight, when he had agreed to leave guns behind, old Joe bore a forty-five stuck in his pants-band.

The tacit leader of the group, Billy Catlin weighed the chances of battle with the Spade men. He shot a glance down the bar. Jess, Packer and the others were debating heatedly. The time was ripe, if they were to do anything.

"Let's go!" he said briefly, hitching up his belt.

The four of them moved toward the door, and in a moment were in the street. Seeing them coming, townsmen walked away, shaking their heads. Just beyond the bar, Bitter Creek spoke up, pausing:

"I don't b'lieve any of Purdy's men are in Mc-Gowan's, boys. It's jest the Spade bunch." He sounded persuasive.

Joe Brush scoffed. "You ascared of 'em, Bitter Crick?"

The latter cooled perceptibly. "D'you think I am, Brush? . . . *I* know what this is goin' to be. We'll go into McGowan's, an' *somebody* ain't comin' back out! If we knock off these Spade boys, the beef-eater'll hire more. If they knock *us* off, there won't be any more!"

"You think there won't!" Len Bain contradicted

sharply. "I tell you, every cowman in the country'll rise on his hind legs if they back us down! D'you think Cheyenne, an' Lusk, an' Med'cine Bow an' them places ain't talkin' about it right now?"

"That's orright too!" Billy thrust in bitterly. " 'Rapahoe's up there, ain't he? Didn't *he* get Glen—him an' Jackson? *They're* my meat! . . . If we c'n nail them, let the cowmen jump in the Platte!"

Bitter Creek nodded grimly. "*We* won't be with 'em, that's all. . . . I've had my howl. Now if we're goin' up there, let's git started!" He had no more to offer, clamping his jaws.

They walked toward McGowan's saloon in a compact body. The eyes of all were on the door in keen anticipation as they went up the steps. Guns were freed in the leather. Joe Brush held his with a nervous grip.

The effect of their entrance was electrical. The bartender faded noiselessly from view behind the bar. A card table crashed as the players lunged for cover. The free-rangers stopped inside the door, staring down the open space at the four Spade men.

Silence held for an aching minute. Arapahoe Jones had whirled to glare like a cornered wolf.

"Name it!" he grated.

For those keyed to striking tension, the suggestion was superfluous. Even Tex O'Malley, who was sure of nothing, didn't want words. He was half-drunk and ugly. He wanted action; and what was more, he would have it.

Van Wagoner was in different case. Vain heroics were foreign to him in this instant. He read the situation keenly, and knew that it was an affair of revenge. Not for nothing had he ferreted out the story of Glen Catlin's shooting. Moreover, he knew that he was drunk; in a condition in which he couldn't trust himself. A pasty hue came over his face as he shrank imperceptibly, feeling behind him for the end of the bar.

Revenge! He knew only too well what that was; how it dragged one through a hell of desire. Revenge was sweet—so long as one lived to savor it! Sweat broke out at his temples as the heart-breaking moment dragged.

Billy Catlin took a step forward, his features predatory. "You don't have to be told, Jones—you or Jackson!" he blazed.

Arapahoe was crouching. He and Billy matched glare for glare. The opposed groups waited for their movement.

It came suddenly. Arapahoe, his visage dark as an Indian's, began to swear in deep, blistering tones; calling Catlin everything he could lay tongue to. Without warning, then, his hand flashed.

Lightning struck in the saloon with stunning decision. Red stabs licked back and forth, vicious and defeaning.

In that first exchange, Arapahoe and Billy shot at each other. Simultaneous with the appearance of the small hole in his forehead, Jones folded up, clattering. Catlin was also mortally hit; but he had strength enough to pump two more slugs into his lifeless enemy.

Others were down. Joe Brush screamed with the agony of a punctured thigh, thrashing over and over. Denny Jackson was doubled over the bar, his head thrown back.

Tex O'Malley, shot by Len Bain, was crawling determinedly forward with an inhuman face, his gun extended and banging. Len finished him ruthlessly, just as a slug in the shoulder sent him reeling.

Powder-smoke was rank in the saloon, hanging in layers which obscured the vision and stung eyes and nostrils. Bitter Creek, dancing about excitedly, snapped the hammer on a dead chamber in his empty six-gun and sprang for the door, dragging Bain with him. None had seen Van Wagoner dodge behind the bar-end at the first explosion. He had known when he was over his head; and he had taken steps.

So it was that the free-rangers from the River Bend, bursting in with Bitter Creek a minute later, behind Jess Catlin, found no trace of Wagoner as they grimly counted the results of the conflict in McGowan's saloon.

Billy Catlin and Arapahoe Jones lay dead on the floor, as did Tex O'Malley; unquestioning, objectless, and game to the last. Joe Brush groaned lustily, lying on his back and clutching his leg. Jackson had passed out, half-hanging on to the bar. Even as they gazed, he slipped off and came down with a sodden crash, his arms flopping.

Jess was in a towering rage. "Dammit!" he flamed in a trembling voice; "Glen gone to hell—an' now Bill! Blood all over the place! . . . An' what good'd it do? Somebody answer me that!"

The free-rangers were silent as they went about their task of removing the combatants from the saloon. Jackson was found to be alive, and laid on the bar. Townspeople came crowding, staring, exclaiming. Some of them ran outside again. The story went down the street like wildfire. By morning it would be hundreds of miles out over the range. The fence war had begun at last.

CHAPTER TWENTY-THREE

RAGGED EDGE

ALTHOUGH it was nearing midday and the scorching sun lay heavy on the roof, Chris Mackey continued to prowl up and down his office at the Spade ranch like a caged beast, as he had done almost without intermission since early morning.

The overseas manager of the Great Plains Cattle Co. shot a glowering look past the office window, the black eye which he had sustained at Casper the night before rendering his aspect baleful. His mood coincided with this appearance exactly, for he had had time since the cold gray dawn to think things over. Now, chafing and delayed, he was savage.

At the window he paused, arrested. A moving dot far off across the tumbled swells of the range held his attention. As the minutes passed, he muttered under his breath, jerking his mutilated cigar from his lips to the floor. Then he returned to his pacing, killing mad.

It was half-an-hour before a bulky form darkened the office door and stepped into the little room, which reeked with stale smoke. As though that evidence of Mackey's impatience warned him, Van Wagoner met his superior with insolent bravado.

"So you decided to come back!" Mackey snapped,

his voice grating. He had not seen the other since the previous night.

"Shore I come back! Did you think I'd be leavin' behind what you owe me? Whut's eatin' you?" Wagoner showed the plain ravages of intoxication in his sagging, grayed jowls.

Mackey turned away, his lips set in a bitter line.

"This is a fine mess!" he rasped, on his next turn. "It's bad enough to get involved with these wolves, without indulging in a gun battle off our own property. Wagoner, I feel as though you were to blame for this fiasco!"

Van snorted. "Blame it on me! You told me——" he began.

"Certainly! I told you what to do! And you very efficiently didn't do it!"

"Wal, from what I hear, 'Rapahoe did hisself proud all alone!" Van argued angrily. "How'd I know I was comin' up against that blasted Swede?"

"And so you tried to—make good, in McGowan's saloon, afterwards?"

Wagoner flung out an arm. "The Swede wasn't there, worse luck! The Tincup laid low. But there's one or two of that Catlin crowd that won't squawk ag'in fer a while!"

Chris's level eye bored into Wagoner. "I suppose you saw nothing of Colonel Purdy's men, then?"

"No, dammit! But if I ever lay hand on Lee——!"

Mackey paused, caught. "You . . . dislike the man, eh?"

Van fumed: "We come up the Texas trail together. An' we'll go to hell together if I can't manage it different!"

The Englishman paced irritably for some moments. "Have you seen Jones since last night?" he queried.

"No. Last I seen 'im, 'Rapahoe was mighty busy."

"And Jackson?" Mackey continued more sharply.

Van shook his head. "Denny's an awful sick man, I'm afeared. He's . . ." He paused.

Mackey withdrew austerely. He was not interested in the grisly details. They made him feel slightly giddy. That a gun fight had taken place in Casper after the cattlemen's meeting he well knew. He did not propose to inquire into the results. They would become apparent in time.

"Van," he said impressively, "I've got a job for you."

Wagoner watched him, his eyes keen.

"This Lee, now," Mackey went on severely. "I don't know what his dirty game is. I could handle Colonel Purdy all right. But Lee seems likely to corner us if we don't do something about it! Do you know what he had the nerve to propose last night? . . . Never mind. I won't have it! That man's got to be stopped!"

"An' so," Wagoner put in ponderously and practically, "you want me to stop 'im?"

Mackey swung on him with that false frankness which denotes lurking uncertainty.

"Damn you, Wagoner—not if you're going to botch the thing! Do you hear me?"

Van eyed him stolidly. "I hear you, all right!" he rumbled significantly. "Damn me, Mackey, an' you damn yoreself! Yo're puttin' me up to rubbin' a man out now, an' it makes my job different. Do you get that?" His manner hardened to grimness. "Go right on talkin', feller!"

He had read Mackey correctly. The Spade manager exploded into unconscious nervousness. He returned to his pacing, his hands active.

"Why, of course I know what you are driving at," he began. He attempted to match Wagoner's rocky hardness, stopping before him and gazing sternly. "How much do you insist on for the—job?"

Wagoner sneered. "Awful cagy, ain't you? . . . Maybe tight is what I mean!"

Mackey flushed. "*You* don't have to go at it that way either!" he fired back.

"Hell I don't! This is yore fix, not mine!" Van snorted through his nostrils fiercely. "Don't think yo're gettin' anything on me! It won't stick . . . Why don't *you* go after the feller?"

Chris Mackey's manner became clipped. "Because I've got to stay here, and you haven't. . . . Will a hundred dollars do you?"

Wagoner stared at him wickedly. "I guess," he said finally; "if that's all yore big syndicate can dig up. But don't think it's the money, Mackey! I've got more in my jeans right now than you've got in yore damn safe!"

Mackey nodded his deliberate assent. "I see. Case of—revenge, you might say." He did not want Van to get thinking about the money he had in the safe, for he did not trust him.

"You c'n call it that."

"Perhaps that will insure results, then, if the money does not."

Van towered over him, suddenly grim, reading his thought. "See yere, you blasted British squirt! Don't you git gay with me! Savvy?"

Gazing up at him with steady pupils, which seemed to shrink, Mackey answered in a small voice: "I—understand you."

"Wal, see you do!"

Wagoner's braggadocio echoed in the little office after the cotton screen had slammed behind him. Mackey stood in the middle of the floor for some time, his gaze lowered. He knew that he was dealing with deadly forces.

He shook his head angrily, and going to his desk, took from it a liquor bottle, to the contents of which he helped himself liberally. It was not one of the times when he smacked his lips with satisfaction afterwards. Nor did he go to the window to watch Van Wagoner ride away on his mission.

The latter, however, was not taking the occasion as seriously as his employer. His was a task that afforded him distinct pleasure in anticipation, and he signalized it by inhaling and releasing great plumes of smoke from his cigarette as he jogged away from the Spade layout on a fresh mount, his Winchester ready to hand in the saddle-boot and his eyes keen under the down-tilted Stetson. Wagoner had not forgotten his wasted chance to get San Saba Lee, two days ago. Every time he thought of the Tincup foreman there came gushing back all his baffled rage against the man.

To his way of thinking, Lee was possessed of unprecedented gall in remaining in this country. "He's got comin' everything he'll git, fer hangin' around Wyomin'!" he thought angrily. "I ain't forgot him makin' an outlaw of me!"

He saw his enforced outlawry as a result of San Saba's sending back to Texas the story of Van's "hard luck" at the roulette wheel, as he had no doubt the other had done. "I'd'a made that up; I know I would!" he argued to himself. As proof of this he presented to himself the fact that in a belt around his waist at the present moment was more money than he had originally lost, and made in the same manner.

"Nosir!" he decided afresh, his jaw brutal. "I won't make it up with Ol' Cap an' Ball! He's out fer believin' that yarn! All the settlin' I'll do will be with Lee—an' blame pronto!"

Wagoner was riding along the Tincup boundary of the Spade ranch now. He turned his pony in the direction of the forlorn grave of Gene Rule beside the north drift fence, wondering how he was to manage his commission.

His scrutiny, darting ahead as he rode, picked out figures far away. He drew in and watched for minutes, judging it to be Tincup cowboys repairing the recently smashed fence. He was not sure, however; for whoever it was did not dismount. There were two of the riders.

Van's eyes narrowed. "One of them's most bound to be Lee!" he growled exultantly. He began to cast about for means of approaching without too early discovery. He had no intention of fighting it out in the open.

Circumstance favored him. A quarter-mile away, and angling across the range until it approached the fence intersections, was a dry gully. It was not deep—only five or six feet in spots—but by bending over in his saddle he could keep concealed.

Accordingly he sought the gully and pushed down it watchfully. His rifle was at the ready now. No one spying him would have been misled as to his object.

San Saba and Colonel Purdy, however, were on the lookout for no such lurking dangers. Their apprehensions were all for the north, and they cast occasional glances in that direction as they estimated the extent of the damage to their fence.

"I think you'h all wrong, San Saba," Colonel Dick argued amiably, a furrow knitting his fine brows. "See how quiet it is—nothin' in any direction." His hand swept the horizon spaciously. "I see Christopher has

already repai'ed his wire," he added, nodding. "No
. . . I think last night's uproar has quieted eve'yone
for the time being. You'll see no more high-jinx for a
right smart while." He smiled hopefully, and added:
"Lend me a match, seh."

San Saba was provoked. "You keep sayin' that,
Kunnel Dick. Can't you *feel* the boil an' bubble undeh
the surface? I tell you——"

He leaned back in his saddle as he spoke, handing
the match over, and his words were cut off cleanly
by the flat echo of a rifle report.

Reaching forward, Colonel Purdy gasped and
sagged out of the saddle as though pushed from behind. As he went, face down, his heel caught on the
near cinch and hung, suspended.

"Good Lo'd!"

San Saba was out of the saddle in a flash. His sharp
gaze across the bay's withers revealed only the
shredded puff of white two hundred yards away on
Spade territory. Listening intently, he heard the
diminishing crack of a horse's hoofs and knew that
the assassin was fleeing.

Then he turned over Colonel Dick, whose pony had
not moved a step. The Colonel was not badly wounded.
His head was furrowed from the temple back along the
skull. Blood ran down his lined cheek in a sheet. His
face was pale, and he was unconscious.

San Saba stood up, blazing anger filming his sight
darkly. He felt morally certain that the treacherous
shot had been meant for himself. His and Colonel

Dick's heads had been very close together, and he had suddenly leaned.

An hour later, he was lifting the Colonel's limp form down from the saddle before the Tincup ranch house.

"He's all right, ma'am; don't you fret!" he told Miss Purdy, as the Colonel's sister fluttered about, agitated to helplessness. With Pink Robinette, who had come running, sworn heartily, and then turned to, he carried Colonel Dick within and laid him on a settee. Having collected her wits sufficiently, Miss Purdy began to look after the Colonel.

When Colonel Purdy sighed and opened his eyes, San Saba turned away. Striding into the library, he selected a rawhide horsewhip from the wall and started for his mount, testing the whip's weight and flexibility.

"Holy cow! Where're you goin' with that, San Saba?" Pink demanded hoarsely, staring after him.

San Saba met his eye with impersonal and flinty decision. "I'm goin' oveh to Chris Mackey's Spade layout an' talk to him," he answered levelly. "And when I get done, you can take my wo'd for it, it'll be somebody else's Spade ranch!"

Pink's jaw dropped as he stepped to the door and watched the Tincup foreman ride away toward the east, slowly and determinedly, like a man who knows what he is going to do.

CHAPTER TWENTY-FOUR

WAGONER CHANGES HIS MIND

SAN SABA'S spotted bay showed signs of nervousness as the sinuous bull-whip in the Tincup foreman's lean, brown hand snaked out and shredded the tips of sage bushes with a vicious snap.

"Neveh you mind, Two-bits," he told the pony at last. "Theah's nothin' to worry about. This ain't youh party at all."

Two-bit's brisk trot was not an evidence of hurry. For San Saba, time did not exist in the matter which held him at present. He was moved solely by disinterested loyalty to his employer; and the retribution which was to descend on Chris Mackey with the certainty of lightning could not be swerved by a difference of ten minutes one way or another.

Chris Mackey saw San Saba coming while he was yet half-a-mile away. The Spade manager looked up from his brooding speculations beside a horse corral, and with the unerring instinct of trepidation recognized his visitor.

And so Van Wagoner had failed of his urgent and deadly mission! Where was the blundering fool now?

Mackey remained by the corral irresolutely while San Saba drew slowly nearer, the corners of his mouth drawn down. Though it seemed otherwise, the waiting man's scrutiny was on the Texan every moment of that time. Only when San Saba approached sufficiently close to allow of a clear examination of his accoutrement did Mackey move away from the corral, drifting toward the ranch house in a deliberate and insolent stroll.

San Saba's very silence was ominous. He did not call out. In fact, he seemed not to watch ahead with any particular intent. Then Mackey saw the bull-whip uncoil.

He began to hasten toward the ranch house, first with quickened stride, and then in a half-run. Fear dogged his heels. It leaped up in his veins like fire when he glanced around and saw San Saba slip out of the saddle like a man slipping off a table-edge, and start after him.

"You, Mackey," he called out now. "I want to talk to you!"

Mackey did not respond, his dark brows taut in his thin red face. He won to the office door a brace of yards ahead of San Saba, and the cotton screen slammed in the latter's face. The inner door banged shut also, and San Saba kicked it open savagely, the half-engaged bolt ripping out with a splintering crash.

Then Mackey was behind his desk, breathing stertorously, his eyes large and staring, as he faced his pursuer. San Saba's features were set in graven lines; the blacksnake trailed in his deceptively quiet hand.

"Mackey," he said with painful clarity, "can I have

your promise to ride away from here for good—clear out, an' stay away?"

"No!" Mackey blurted thunderously, out of the depths of his fear.

The hand holding the whip moved, and the lash twitched up off the floor, curling. "I'm goin' to give you every chance there is," San Saba said levelly. "It's what I'm doin' right now!" The moderation of the words made Mackey jump.

"Good heavens, man!" Chris burst out, grasping the desk. "What have I done?" His appeal seemed uncannily addressed to an agency beyond either of them in the room.

"No questions!" San Saba warned, unmoved. "No answers—no lies—nothing . . . Are you goin'?" His tone rose suddenly to a snap.

Mackey stared at him, frozen.

"You," San Saba suddenly shot out, bitterly, "are not fit to live in this country. You're not big enough!" His drawl, which had engagingly tinged so many of his arguments, was in the limbo of things to be desired now. "I happen to be deliverin' the verdict. It don't mean a thing, Mackey—me bein' here alone. Tomorrow—some day—somebody'll be doin' this. You had better be glad it's me!"

His voice had dropped to a lashing drone, but it went on without pause: "You are leavin' these parts now. Nobody asks you. I'm tellin' you. You come to this country and you thought it was yours. You thought all you had to do was make your rules—snap

your whip—and men would growl and obey. Do you
get that? Men!" He stared scornfully while it sank in.
"But you are all wrong, Mackey. You don't measure
up. You can't hold a whip! You're not even brave!
And so you go . . . I'm talkin' a lot. I like folks to
understand all that's necessary. Now I'm done."

Mackey stared at him, a muscle in his cheek twitching.

Suddenly the whip streaked out, whistling, and
snaked around Chris' shoulders. He shrieked and staggered; one tension broken, a greater one gripping him.

"No!" he bleated desperately. "I won't go! I
won't——!" He was half-sobbing now, stumbling
around the desk toward the door, blindly, his arms
before his face, though the whip had not touched him
there.

"You will!"

The lash curled around Mackey's legs, almost trip-
ping him. Perspiration dewed San Saba's face at the
necessity to continue.

Mackey was in the door now.

"I'll never!" he screamed abjectly, protesting by
hysterical rote. "I'll never! I'll never!" The cry rang
amongst the ranch buildings weirdly.

Mackey darted toward the barns. San Saba came
after him with grim persistence, the warning crack
of the bull-whip stinging the Spade manager's naked
soul without touching his shrinking flesh.

In the midst of this uproar the spiteful crash of
a rifle from somewhere amongst the buildings went

almost unnoticed. Almost, though not quite; for while neither Mackey nor San Saba were touched by the flying slug, the latter had caught the dull, metallic echo with some part of his attention that was forever on the watch.

He did not pause in his stride, nor did Mackey. Straight toward San Saba's pony the Spade manager bore, half-a-dozen yards ahead of his pursuer.

The bay reared and plunged as Mackey hit the saddle. Then at the man's unearthly howl the pony started away in a dead run, off toward the south. San Saba stopped in his tracks and watched horse and man diminish at an incredible pace.

"That's done," he muttered distastefully, as he dropped the bull-whip like a thing accursed. "Reckon I'll get my pony back, sometime. But if I don't——"

His shrug blended into his gesture of hitching up trousers and cartridge-belt as he swung back toward the Spade ranch house. He knew that despite the other's loud protestations, Chris Mackey would not come back. Time would persuade the outlander to alter his intentions, and he would wind up his affairs in connection with the Spade ranch from Cheyenne or some other convenient point.

"Now I'll see about the rest," San Saba murmured, his keen scrutiny roving the silent structures. The deserted aspect of the ranch was not reassuring, in the light of the shot which he had heard, and which he had no doubt had been meant for himself.

What remained before him he knew to be a vastly

different matter from what he had just come through. No longer would the bull whip of Colonel Purdy be of use. It would be a matter of cold steel and cold nerve, and he experienced some curiosity as to the identity of his adversary.

Arapahoe Jones? He frowned. Not Arapahoe. The latter, whatever his faults, would not have shot from cover. Van Wagoner, then? San Saba was undecided; but something within him leaped at the prospect as he strode in the direction of the bunk room at the other end of the ranch building.

He had thought his animosity against his old trail boss dead, burned to ashes by time and the application of sober sense. It was not. Suddenly, more than anything he wished in his life, San Saba wanted to meet Wagoner again.

He threw open the screen door of the bunk room with a bang. It awakened Colorado, who had been standing guard over the deserted ranch the night before. He leaned forward in his bunk, blinking, while San Saba, his six-gun ready in his grasp, calmly examined the big room for any possible place of concealment. There was none. There was no lurking figure anywhere. Colorado finally said with unction: "That you, San Saba? What you divin' fer?"

San Saba did not answer him. He had already turned back to the door. Colorado sank back, relieved. Then he remembered the gun. He hunkered up, frowning, and scratched his head, staring at the door.

San Saba was uncertain where to look next. He set

off for the corrals and out-buildings, keeping a strict watch ahead. Except for the horses and colts, and the scratching chickens, no life appeared anywhere.

He found the corrals—the tool shed—the black-smith shop—solitary and silent. He was beginning to believe his quarry to have fled incontinently; when coming around the cook shack in his persistent search, he found himself suddenly face to face with Wagoner. The latter was crouched, and in his hands was still the telltale, ready Winchester.

He heard Van's harsh intake of breath in that quiet moment; saw the swift change in his predatory, animal-like gaze. At the same instant that the rifle barrel swung around and belched thunderously, San Saba flung up his forty-five and fired.

He felt a smashing blow in his chest and reeled back, so that he had no further immediate chance to shoot. Shadows, in the midst of the bright glare, over-rode him. Before he was aware that he had lost his balance, the ground struck at him from behind.

Turning his head, he saw that Wagoner was also on the ground, stiffening with pain, his hard features a mask of suffering.

"We cain't shoot—straight," San Saba gasped, roll-ing over with great effort. "Blame you, Wagoneh—I should've got you!"

Wagoner stilled, reason in his eyes as he craned to stare. A small flame leaped there when he saw that San Saba too, had fallen. "You—have got me, Lee!" he got out. "Leastways—I think you have! But I can maybe—git you before I—go!" His body writhed as he struggled to extricate the rifle, which had fallen under him.

"Don't you!" San Saba exclaimed, alarmed. There was no heat in these exchanges; only cool determination. "I'll have to finish you wheah you lay, Van, if you try! I don't want to do that."

Van groaned and desisted. "If I can't, I—can't," he breathed gustily. "But damn you, Lee—I almost had you!"

"You did fo' a fact, Van! But right was against you. You couldn't've won, man!" He struggled up on an elbow. "Plumb th'ough the breather!" he panted, as blood frothed his lips. "But I'll pull out of it—if I can—stop this bleedin'. Wheah's that blasted—Colorado?" Things grew black before him then, and he lay back.

Wagoner thought darkly for fleeting moments, arrested by something San Saba had said. Was it true? Had it been *right* that was against him, from the first? When Colorado peered around the corner of the bunk room a minute later he was held back by the sight of Van's desperate efforts. He thought the man to be fighting for his gun.

"Lee!" Van growled at last. "Lee!"

San Saba strove back through fainting dreams to turn his eyes. Sweat stood out in beads on Van Wagoner's brow, but he was staring across, intent.

"There's the double-damned cash—blast you!" Van ground out shortly, laboriously flipping toward San

Saba the money belt which he had painfully won from around his middle. "You win—Ol' Cap an' Ball gets his money. There's more'n enough there. I—changed my mind!"

San Saba's blue eyes, seeming to reflect the limpid sky, widened as he read in the words the long struggle in the other's soul which had only just been decided.

"Van! You mean——" he stumbled, warmed by something not blood nor sun; "you'h payin' back——?"

"Shet—up!" Van growled, with a last burst of spirit. His graying face was as tight, as dour and harsh, as it would ever be; but his glance was half-ashamed. "I'm wore out! I—changed my mind, 'sall! Now lemme . . . sleep.

"Van!" San Saba called weakly, wearily.

He received no answer, and presently lay back again as though reflecting.

When Colorado made his cautious way forward after minutes of silence, he saw at once that Van Wagoner, like Christopher Mackey, but by a faster means, had taken the long, straight trail away from the Spade ranch at last.

San Saba lay unconscious, blood beading his lips and crusting his cotton shirt; on his pale face a look of renewed discovery; and in his clenched hand a worn and heavy money belt, like a reprieve.

CHAPTER TWENTY-FIVE

SPADE WORK

SAN SABA lay at the Spade ranch at the point of death for a matter of days. The surgeon who rode out from the Fort to attend him would not permit his removal. San Saba was not himself in a condition to know where he was.

As the Tincup foreman had predicted, Chris Mackey did not come back. After a perplexed period of amiable bickering between Colorado, another remaining cowboy, the cook, and the male nurse sent out by the surgeon to look after San Saba, there appeared at the ranch an authoritative, business-like gentleman in whip-cords, with a scrutinizing gaze behind thick glasses, who said he was an American trustee from Omaha.

At Cheyenne this man had received "instructions" as to conditions from Chris Mackey before the latter's hasty departure for England. He wisely did not press his investigation further through inadvised questions, except for riding over the range in company with Colorado and asking brief and practical things concerning the working of stock.

Surprised into respect, Colorado answered so well that he was given three more cowboys and left in the position of temporary foreman, which was not at all good for the size of his hat-band.

The man from Omaha, Vance by name, spent two more days mainly in the company of Colonel Purdy, on the Tincup. There he heard the story of the past two weeks at first-hand, and made his plans accordingly; after which, having left orders with Colorado, he departed once more in the direction of Nebraska.

In that brief visit, however, had been planted the seeds of peace concerning the range dispute. On the first day that San Saba was permitted to visit as he willed, he received much news of interest concerning this and other things, and some that gave him pain; both from Colorado, who stopped in to cuss him smilingly any number of times, and from Colonel Purdy, who visited him shortly before noon of that day.

He was gratified to learn that the trustee from Omaha had unconditionally approved the proposal for a half-mile-wide cattle lane between the two ranches; and that during the doubtful period of his recuperation, the fencing of the lane had not only been begun, but speedily finished.

San Saba thus experienced the sober pleasure of awakening to the full accomplishment of his relinquished dream.

"I plainly told Mist' Vance that he could thank you for whateveh trouble and money it saved us, too," Colonel Dick made clear. "I explained to him the dark outlook for us othehwise, and he agreed with me. Theah's nothing like credit wheah credit *is* due." He said it as though it were still a source of astonishment that San Saba's original proposal had been adopted.

The latter, however, appeared mainly interested in the acceptance of the compromise by the free-rangers. He plied Colorado with persistent queries, and pondered the replies for long intervals, seeking therein the answers to questions of his own. Colorado artlessly dropped into his mind the unwinnowed gleanings of the past two or three days.

"Bandy Packer drove through yestidy," he announced, "an' Chiles an' *his* bunch a couple hours behind him. 'Nother small outfit went through sometime in the night. They want to git down onto the south graze fer a couple weeks or so before they ship; an' still they'll make the early market, fat an' slick! . . . The boys visited with me fer near an hour. It don't take many hands to git through that fenced lane . . . They tell me," Colorado went on, eager to inform, "that Catlin is drivin' through some time today. I hear Jess is fed up with fence, though. Figures to take a bunch up into Montana fer the winter, an' mebbe ship over the Northern Pacific next year. Some of the old stockmen're bound to drift off. But more'll take their place."

Yes, San Saba thought, that was what Jess Catlin would do—drift away, farther ahead of barbed-wire and growing population. After all, the man was a free ranger, bred to it through the years. And with him would go Rhoda, seeking new scenes, smiling gravely at other men; meeting life as bravely as she had always met it.

He could not blame her for an active distaste toward the scene and associations of her brothers' death. Nor could he expect her to be appreciative of a conclusion to the range dispute which really had been little more than an accident.

No! Concession though it was, the cattle lane had all along been the unquestionable right of the free-rangers. One could not expect any of them, much less Rhoda, to be grateful for something for which they had both fought and given life.

He would see Rhoda no more. He repeated that to himself over and over again. He received unquestionable confirmation of his loss from an unexpected visitor who popped gayly in while his nurse was gathering up the dishes of his noon meal. It was, of all persons, Belle Hammond, on her way back to Fetterman from Medicine Bow.

"Well, well!" she exclaimed, panting from the exertion of climbing out of a wagon and walking through the ranch house. "This is a fine note for the lovelorn cowboy—taking to his bed! For grief, I daresay?" She disseminated an antiseptic cynicism, twitching his bedcovering straight wth competent brusquery.

San Saba sheared to the essential question with sober directness. "Belle, I sho' gummed things up with Rhoda Catlin, that day. I hadn't a chance to come and tell you. . . . Did you eveh see her again?"

"Did I!" Belle chuckled understandingly. She told

him how Rhoda had come by chance almost directly to her, and how *she* had spilled the beans in her turn. She recounted something of Rhoda's vehemence in rejecting her invitation. "Well," she ended practically, "it didn't overly matter, San Saba. Everything seemed to stop from that day, far as she was concerned. And it wouldn't have done *you* any good. She . . ." Belle hesitated. "You'll not see her again, San Saba. I expect you know that." She gazed at him levelly, measuring his reaction, compassion deep in her eyes while she struck the clean, merciful blow.

"Ye-es," he said slowly, "I expect I know that." His eyes dropped to the blanket.

She told him a little of what Rhoda had said about him in her distraction. But San Saba had had enough. She could get no more out of him, and presently left, unoffended.

"There's another visitor here anyway, that'll maybe please you better!" She slipped out as the other entered.

"Rhoda—ma'am!" San Saba exclaimed, or tried to exclaim; for his throat, his chest, suddenly burned with a prickling fire which overflowed into his eyes and blinded them.

She came toward him without embarrassment, and sank on the edge of the bed, her steady gaze on his face. Her brows were drawn, her lips firm-pressed; but he thought he had never seen her look so beautiful.

"San Saba! I never knew—I only heard this morning . . . But you are so husky! Do not speak—lie still. You are all right?" Her voice was a benediction, liquid and kind. Her hands, on her lap, did not appear overly composed.

"All right," he assented, smiling wanly. "I can talk now, a little. Why! It is mo' than two weeks ago . . . Rhoda, what I can neveh unde'stand is why youh people didn't come down heah the next day, after that Caspeh—business, an' wipe us out, fence and all! Maybe you can tell me."

He had, he recognized now, after-all wanted to hear this from her—an unexpected reward for what little he had been able to do.

She was staring at him in puzzlement. "Don't you know? San Saba, I . . . But you went home that night, as you would—as all of them should have done!" She appeared to contemplate for a melancholy moment. "Has no one told you that there was a gun battle that night in Casper, later on—and that three men were killed, and several others wounded? It occurred in McGowan's saloon, and nothing was settled by it; absolutely nothing. But it put a different face on everything for some time to come."

"Wounded—killed!" he whispered, deeply stirred. "I ce'tainly should have known! Rhoda . . . who?"

She met his searching gaze gamely. "Arapahoe Jones was killed outright, San Saba; and a man named O'Malley, a Texan. And Billy . . ."

"You poor girl!" he got out, moved to strong compassion. "Glen first. And now . . ."

"Joe Brush was badly wounded, but is recovering.

Denny Jackson, also . . . I heard about Colonel Purdy, and Mr. Mackey, and Wagoner—and you," she burst out, then. "But only today, San Saba! I would surely have come sooner. I . . . Jess has told me about that day at our camp; how you saved me, saved us both, from certain death," she went on in a lower tone, her eyes sinking. "I feel differently about that—now. I did not know those men then. I did not dream . . ."

Perspiration stood out on San Saba's brow as he recognized thankfully that he would not have to explain his motives during that trying experience, to her or to anyone. Jess had understood. He had understood generously. And now Rhoda did also.

"But tell me how the free-rangehs took it when the fence was opened," he prompted huskily, endeavoring to swing her mind away from the darker aspects of the past.

She told him how Colonel Purdy, after his swift recovery, the consultation with Vance, and the decision to concede, had ridden to Fetterman and sought out the free-rangers, man by man; how he had parleyed with them afresh, and this time mollified them with promises that were kept.

"I must admit," Rhoda said bravely, "that his task was made considerably easier in the—absence of most of the hot-heads. After the Casper shooting, things were quiet for a space. But I believe they would not have gone on so, if it had not been for the solution which you—forced, San Saba, in the face of us all!"

San Saba shook his head over the story. "I am ce'tainly sorry about the whole thing, ma'am; I most ce'tainly am! I wish I could've been on youh side. I would have gone straight to Mackey befo'—anything had happened."

Rhoda enlivened at this, fixing on him a bright look of inquiry. "Oh, San Saba—I so wanted you to be . . . elsewhere! *Why* wouldn't you give it up, go with your convictions and your friends?"

He saw now that the answer meant more to her than he had dreamed it would.

"Why! Don't you know?" he smiled in his turn. Without ado he told her the story of the trail herd belonging to his uncle, which had come up from Texas in Van Wagoner's care; how Wagoner had gambled away the money realized on the cattle; and how he had taken the best job he could find, grimly determined to make good his uncle's loss.

"And that's not all of it eitheh," he told her shyly, but with pale resolution. "Theah was no necessity fo' me to do it, except within myself—something I'll always answeh to, ma'am. I wanted in the wo'st way to quit and follow my . . . inclinations, I'll call it. But I made up my mind theah wasn't no pa't of a man about a fello' who'd do it that way, and I stuck. I'm not sorry," he added doggedly, his blue eyes serene and sincere under the sorrel thatch. "I'd do it all oveh again, I reckon."

Touched to her heart, Rhoda felt the power and honesty of this slim man like an impact. She withdrew her gaze hastily from his and took refuge in what she could subscribe to with vehemence—indignation.

"What a shame that such things can happen to anyone!" she exclaimed, her cheeks reddening. "Certainly you could not have let it be known in the circumstances you found yourself in. But at the same time——"

"Ah, but that ain't all of it, ma'am!" he interrupted her gently, with satisfaction. "Van Wagoneh was mistaken an' wrong—but he ce'tainly wasn't all bad." He drew from beneath his pillow a clinking, rustling money-belt. "He gave me this the day he—checked in, ma'am. Mo' than enough to pay what was gambled away. The first thing I am goin' to do when I get on my laigs again will be to send Old Cap and—that is, my uncle, what he has due him. The rest will just about make up what I sent back of my own money in the meantime." He lay thinking contentedly, and yet sadly. "Poor old Van, he——"

"And so what are you going to do now, San Saba?" Rhoda inquired in a tone she strove to make casual. "Now that you are free."

His warm smile was quick and airy. "Why, I don't know, Rho—ma'am, I mean. I was thinkin' of askin' advice. Of cou'se there's the wide world I've yet to see." He paused, while she looked at him fleetingly, and then went on:

"But heah's the funniest thing. You'd neveh in the world guess! . . . It seems the Great Plains Co., the English concern that owned this Spade ranch, was already in negotiation with some American buyers, without anyone knowin' about it. This fello' Vance, from Omaha, is one of the new ownehs; and I heah he is a fine man.

"Well, it seems," he went on whimsically, "that Chris Mackey had already been found slightly disappointin', and one of Mist' Vance's objects was to find a satisfactory manager fo' the ranch. So he asked Kunnel Purdy fo' a recommend, an' blame that Tennessee rascal if he didn't go fo' to name me! I don't know how to take it—whetheh Kunnel Dick got to thinkin' I was runnin' him, or what—though I suspect he was so pleased with gettin' rid of Mackey that he just decided to appoint his own choice of a successor and run no risks!"

Rhoda was gazing at him with glowing eyes—eyes only a little questioning, under the fetching brown hair. "And you will accept, San Saba?"

"Why—now, theah you have me!" he admitted artfully. His hand had crept imperceptibly towards hers on the blanket. It now lifted, and came down softly, over her own. "You see—what I don't know about this kind of a ranch is a shame!"

"San Saba!" Rhoda exclaimed reproachfully. She had not moved her hand, except flutteringly. Her color was high.

"No! That is a fact!" he persisted. "I'd sho'ly need

he'p on a ranch like this—with chickens, and ducks, and the like. I—I'm most nea'ly afraid to tackle it alone!"

He was gently, insistently pleading now, his blue eyes seeking to hold her hazel ones. Her soft face tugged at his heart alarmingly; he had the baffling sense of indulgence in insuperable folly. She would never have such a one as him!

Rhoda half-rose, her head turned toward the door, pretending to be startled at the threatened approach of someone. It was a false alarm, however. She sank back, rosy and self-conscious; but curiously collected too, as she gazed at him the unspoken question which is in every maid's heart.

"Ma'am—Rhoda——" he began afresh, never releasing his hold on her small brown hand; *"may* I call you Rhoda?" he pressed on impulsively, having broken off another intended query, and watching her.

"If you—wish," she got out, meeting his eyes with a look such as he had never seen before.

"No, but—I mean—foreveh, ma'am!" he exclaimed in earnest trepidation, his own brow and throat now reddening duskily with the difficulty of the vital question. He had never done anything harder than this.

"You red-headed Texas tease—yes!" she answered muffledly, her face buried in that sorrel mop; for he had pulled her to him masterfully at last, and she had come.

"And so, shall we accept Omaha's offeh—together,

girl?" he insisted, his heart standing still while he waited.

"Foreveh—boy!" she imitated him roguishly, turning her flushed face to his.

"Good! We'll begin ouh Spade wo'k as soon as eveh I am able. That's what it'll be, too. Spade wo'k for a real foundation! You have made me ve'y happy . . . ma'am!"

The rest was silence.

THE END